PRAISE

the HANNAH WEST SERIES,

by LINDA JOHNS:

Book 1, *Hannah West in the Belltown Towers*:

"Johns has concocted a wonderful character in twelve-year-old Hannah West, who wanders the street, closely observing her surroundings. Adopted from China as an infant, Hannah and her adoptive mother, an artist, earn their way by house-sitting, with Hannah making extra money as a dog walker and errand runner. [A] great backstory and an engaging heroine . . ." —*Booklist*

"[A] delightful mystery." —*Children's Literature*

Book 2, *Hannah West in Deep Water*:

"Hannah is inquisitive, lively, and outspoken, and her often-droll first-person narrative incorporates plenty of local flavor, as well as a growing awareness of marine conservation issues." —*Booklist*

"Linda Johns creates a convincing setting with plenty of detail about her hometown. Hannah is an appealing protagonist, who unravels the mystery efficiently, but with enough bumps along the way to be satisfying. This is fiction that is both fun and educational."

—*Children's Literature*

Book 3, *Hannah West in the Center of the Universe*: Selected as a **Global Reading Challenge Book**.

Book 4, *Hannah West on Millionaire's Row*:

"There is something irresistible about a young, precocious sleuth. Hannah West is no exception, adding a modern Northwestern twist to the age-old formula. [F]ans will like Hannah's breezy tone and upbeat personality, and they'll appreciate her love of dogs and books, and the copious details she offers about life in Seattle . . . [G]irls looking for a brainy, modern-day Trixie Belden will find Hannah West a contender."

—*Booklist*

HANNAH WEST

SLEUTH IN TRAINING

By Linda Johns

two lions

two lions

Text copyright © 2006 Linda Johns
Introduction copyright © 2016 Nancy Pearl

Published by Two Lions, New York

www.apub.com

Amazon, the Amazon logo, and Two Lions are trademarks of Amazon.com, Inc., or its affiliates.

This book was originally published as two volumes,
Hannah West and the Belltown Towers and *Hannah West in Deep Water*.

ISBN-13: 9781503947160 (hardcover)
ISBN-10: 1503947165 (hardcover)
ISBN-13: 9781503946941 (paperback)
ISBN-10: 1503946940 (paperback)

Cover art © 2016 Michael S. Heath
Book design by Virginia Pope

Printed in the United States of America

With gratitude to
Nancy Pearl
and
Nancy Johns Heard

CONTENTS

INTRODUCTION

When I was a kid I read the first thirty-four Nancy Drew mysteries, in order, from *The Secret of the Old Clock* to *The Hidden Window Mystery*. Truth be told, I am not sure now, looking back, why I kept reading them. I had no desire at all to be a detective, and didn't much identify with Nancy and her chums. At the same time I also read the first thirteen novels in the Dana Girls series, also by Carolyn Keene, the author of the Nancy Drew mysteries, as well as every other mystery that I could find, including the long-running series starring Frank and Joe Hardy.

My love for mysteries has continued unabated throughout my life, and I am always on the lookout for new ones to read, whether they're aimed at adults, teens, or children. When I moved to Seattle, children's librarians and booksellers kept telling me how much kids enjoyed the four mysteries featuring a twelve-year-old Chinese-American detective named Hannah West. And once I read them I could see why. Hannah is smart, brave, and resourceful; the mysteries she solves are both complex and interesting. Starting with *Hannah West in the Belltown Towers*, these are perfect for eight- to twelve-year-olds who love realistic fiction.

I was thrilled to have the opportunity to interview Linda Johns about writing the Hannah West novels on page 285.

—**Nancy Pearl**

BOOK ONE

HANNAH WEST
in the
BELLTOWN
TOWERS

CHAPTER 1

YOU MIGHT THINK I'd feel a little triumphant, having gone from homeless twelve year old to cushy downtown high-rise girl overnight. But mostly I was thirsty. This whole moving thing was getting tiresome, even when it meant moving up.

This time we really were moving up—up to the eleventh floor in Belltown Towers. It was my sixth move this year— six moves in sixth grade.

"Buck up, it's our last trip," Mom said. She put her laptop bag down on top of a wheeled suitcase.

"Water . . . need water," I said dramatically. I held up a plastic bag that was serving as transportation for Vincent and Pollock, my two goldfish.

Moving had become a ritual for Mom and me. We always saved a few things for the last trip. Our most precious belongings, Mom said. For her, that was her laptop computer, a painting by her friend Nina, and a small box of photographs (featuring yours truly). For me, it was my sketch pad, three big drawings I did last summer at the Y's

Art for All camp, a wooden box of 120 color pencils, and a framed photo of me and my best friend, Lily, at the beach. And Vincent and Pollock, of course.

"Hold the elevator!" an older woman with a little dog called from the front door. Her dog reminded me of a silver-tipped version of Toto from *The Wizard of Oz*.

"I'm afraid there's nothing to hold yet," Mom said. "We're still waiting for the elevator."

The woman sighed. Her little dog plopped down into a sit, as if he were sighing, too. "This elevator is impossibly slow," she said. "I find it so inconvenient."

Uh-oh. My Snoot Alert went into active mode. Owen had told us that everyone in Belltown Towers knew one another. This woman was probably wondering what we were doing walking into her swanky building with armloads of stuff. She looked pretty swanky herself. Her salt-and-pepper hair perfectly matched her dog's coat, which somehow made more of a statement than my purple high-tops, which I'd thought tied in nicely with the purple Concrete Jungle logo on my black skateboard T-shirt. I had a sinking feeling that we wouldn't fit in at Belltown Towers at all.

But then the woman smiled. "Hello, dear," she said to me. "It seems Ruff is quite interested in your drawings. Or your fish."

The little dog was sniffing and nuzzling me. I bent down to get some dog kisses while Mom rushed into her customary introductions.

"Hello, I'm Maggie West, and this is my daughter, Hannah," Mom said. She always tries to get to know people as soon as possible when we get to a new place. She says the more people we know, the more people will look out for us. "We're taking care of Owen Henderson's place while he's in Nepal."

"We're taking care of his fish, too," I added.

"Oh, of course," the woman said. "Owen told me about his house sitters. He also told me that a certain young miss is excellent with all kinds of pets, not just the aquatic variety."

"I love animals," I said, scratching Ruff on his belly. "He's a cairn terrier, right? Just like Toto?"

She laughed. "Yes, indeed. Not many people realize that Toto was a cairn. You must really know dogs." She looked at me again. "Dear, do you mind if I ask you something?"

Uh-oh. I knew what was coming now. I braced myself. She was definitely older than Grandma. Maybe even as old as GG (my great-grandma). She might be the kind who would ask, "Are you Oriental?" Lots of old people say "Oriental" for anything they think might have ties anywhere in the huge continent of Asia, including mu shu pork, sushi, and teriyaki chicken. But maybe she would be one of those people who just blurts out, "What are you?" because they can't tell someone from Korea or China apart. It makes me feel like a freak when someone asks me "what" I am like that.

The answer, in case you're wondering, is that I'm

Chinese. But my mom isn't. She adopted me from China when I was six months old. It's not that unusual to be a girl from China adopted by non-Chinese parents, especially here in Seattle. Still, some people—usually the older kind of people—just aren't used to it.

But I digress. Mom brought me back to the present with a look that said, *Use your manners, Hannah.*

I took a deep breath and let it out, which turned out to be a bit of a sputter to blow some wisps of my ultrastraight hair out of my face. It's not the most sophisticated move, but it helps me think while I buy time. "Ask me anything you'd like," I said. I didn't really mean it. Clearly no one ever means it when they say "ask me anything."

"Well, dear, I'm having a little health trouble right now, and the doctor wants me to take it easy for a few days. I'm looking for someone to walk Ruff and make sure he gets enough exercise. Would you be interested in a dog-walking job? Owen highly recommended you," she said. "Of course, I need to make sure it's agreeable to your mother," she quickly added.

Mom nodded with a smile and I laughed. I hadn't been expecting that one at all. "I'd love to be Ruff's dog walker," I said. "And you can walk me, little guy," I said, scratching behind his perky ears. I reached into the back pocket of my shorts and pulled out a card. Some of my friends think it's totally dorky that I have business cards. But let me tell you, these things come in handy.

I handed one to the woman.

Hannah J. West

Pet Sitter, Dog Walker,
Plant Waterer, and
all around Errand Girl

235-6628

"I can give you references, if you need them. And that's my cell-phone number. You can reach me there," I said.

The woman read my card and gave a little chuckle. "A cell phone, eh?"

"We're professional house sitters," Mom rushed in to say. I think she was afraid I'd seem spoiled because I have a cell phone when the truth is that we're technically homeless. "I got a great deal on a family plan, so Hannah and I each have a cell phone. It makes it easy for our families to reach us when we're moving from house to house, with all our house-sitting jobs."

"Well then, that's a good idea. I think it's great for a young girl living in the city to have a phone with her," the woman said. "You can keep in touch with your mom and call for help if you run into trouble, which I'm sure you don't." She gave me a wink.

The elevator doors opened, and a man and a woman navigating a huge jogging stroller got off. "Sorry for hogging the elevator, Dorothy," the woman said.

Dorothy smiled warmly at them and said, "You certainly have your hands full." The three of us (four, if you count Ruff; six, if you count Vincent and Pollock, but I've noticed people don't usually count fish) got on the elevator.

"Oh dear. I neglected to introduce myself. I'm Dorothy. Dorothy Powers."

I thought I heard Mom gasp a little.

"You've already met Ruff, of course," Dorothy went on. "It seems my little companion has taken quite a liking to you, Hannah. Usually it takes a bit of a treat to win him over, but it appears he instinctively understands you're his ticket to walks in the great outdoors."

Ruff gave a little yelp when she said "walk." Just to test him, I looked at him and said, "Walk?" He yelped again.

"Sorry. Couldn't help myself," I said, feeling a bit foolish for having teased my new canine client. I pushed *11* on the elevator panel, feeling the Braille spots above it just to luxuriate in the idea of living up so high.

"Thirteen, please," Dorothy said.

I looked at the number panel. There were buttons going up to twelve, but no thirteen. Above twelve there was a button that said "ph."

"It's the one that says *ph*, dear," Dorothy said.

"Why doesn't it just say thirteen?" I asked, pressing the "ph" button for her.

"It's an old superstition," Dorothy said. "Even though this is a new building, it's a little old-fashioned. You see, some people used to be afraid of the number thirteen. No one wanted to live on the thirteenth floor. So landlords would pretend there wasn't a thirteenth story. They'd skip right from twelve to fourteen."

"But then fourteen would really be thirteen. Wouldn't that be unlucky, too?" I asked.

"One would think so, if one believed such things. I've been living on what is really the thirteenth floor for three years now, and I haven't had any bad luck," she said. "In fact, I wish they'd just call it thirteen and be done with it. Penthouse is a bit uppity for my taste, especially since the Belltown Towers calls both top-floor apartments penthouse. But I do love my apartment. You must come see it sometime. In fact, I have a new Hansen painting arriving today. I'd love to show it to you both."

We reached the eleventh floor, and Mom and I maneuvered our loads out into the hallway, trying not to get shut in the elevator doors.

"It was such a pleasure to meet you," Mom gushed.

I looked at Mom. She was practically beaming she looked so excited.

"It was lovely meeting you both," Dorothy called.

"You, too," I said. And I really meant it. I'd totally underestimated Dorothy. I'd been so caught up worrying about myself and whether she would call me "Oriental" that I almost hadn't given her a fair chance. My GG would say I was being ageist by assuming someone over seventy was going to be out of touch or, worse, as GG would say herself, "a culturally insensitive bigot."

"See you later, Ruff!" I called out just before the elevator doors closed completely.

I couldn't wait for my new dog-walking job. Not only would it be nice to have a furry animal to hang out with downtown, I'd be making some much-needed cash.

"Ohmygod ohmygod ohmygod!" Mom said as she fumbled for the key to number 1105, Owen's apartment. I mean OUR apartment. "Do you have any idea who we just met?"

CHAPTER 2

AS SOON AS she got the door open, Mom started bustling around the apartment like a crazy woman. Which she is, sometimes. I mean, not really crazy. But she gets pretty excited over weird things.

I went straight into the kitchen. I needed to get Vincent and Pollock into a bowl of fresh water as soon as possible. All this moving every few weeks must be unsettling for the little guys.

"Do you have any idea who we just met?" Mom asked again.

Well, I thought I did, but now I was wondering if I'd missed something. "Who?" I demanded.

"Dorothy Powers!"

Sometimes it's so hard not to just blurt "Well, duh!" to a parent. But I speak from experience when I say that those two seemingly harmless syllables work overtime when it comes to annoying adults.

"Okay..." I stalled for time. The name didn't ring any bells to me. "So, who is she, besides the owner of my new client?"

"Dorothy Powers just happens to be one of the top three art supporters in Seattle! She has an incredible collection of art and a wonderful eye for new talent. If Dorothy Powers is behind you, you have it made as an artist," she said.

"Good. Maybe she'll discover me, and I'll be able to rent our old house back again," I said. My sarcasm went unnoticed.

"Owen told me she lived in this building. But I had no idea she'd be so nice. Or that we'd meet her our first day here. Our first hour here! Or that she'd invite us to her apartment! Did you hear her say that she's getting a new Hansen?" Mom fumbled in her purse for her phone. "I need to call Nina right away!" Mom headed out to the balcony with her cell phone. I whipped mine out, too. If she was going to call her best friend, then I'd call mine.

"If you're hearing this message, it means you should leave a message right after this . . . *beep*."

"Hey, Lily. Hannah here. If you want to call me, you can reach me in my downtown, totally happenin' condo. Later."

Lily had said she was envious of Mom and me being part of some schmaltzy *Lifestyles of the Rich and Famous* type of TV show, getting to stay in fancy houses and downtown high-rises. But I know she was just saying that to make me feel better, because the truth is I'd give anything to be back in our old house in the Maple Leaf neighborhood with my best friend just down the street, instead of six miles up the freeway.

And the rest of the truth is that I wasn't lying when I said we were technically homeless. I know, I know—it could be a lot worse. A LOT worse.

Here's the sixteen-word *Reader's Digest* version of what happened: Mom got laid off. We ran out of money. We started house-sitting instead of paying rent.

Here's the one-hundred-sixty-four-word version, for those who like a little more detail: Mom got laid off from her job at MegaComp. She tried to find a job at another dot-com company, but everyone was cutting back.

Someone with Mom's background—art history major, art critic, and writer—wasn't exactly in demand in Seattle's job market. She took a part-time job at Wired coffee shop and started freelance writing, but neither pays much. We had to make some serious cuts in how much money we spent. First we cut back on pizza deliveries. Then we canceled cable. We rented out a bedroom in our house to a college student. We had three yard sales. We held on as long as we could. Finally, we sold everything that wouldn't fit in our 1999 Honda Civic. One of Mom's old bosses at MegaComp let us stay at her house while she went on a four-week vacation. That was when Mom got the great idea of being professional house sitters, which is a lot better than being amateur homeless people.

Luckily, Mom is one of those people who knows a lot of people, including people who happen to be rich. Luckily, those rich people travel a lot—and they all like Maggie

West. So it was natural for them to hire West House-Sitting Services to take care of their houses and pets while they bicycled around Scotland or went to cooking school in the south of France or climbed Mount Kilimanjaro or did whatever it is rich people do on their vacations. They head out to see the world; we get to stay in Seattle rent-free.

The best house-sitting gigs are the ones that last at least four weeks. This time, we'd totally scored. We'd be at Belltown Towers, complete with a view of the water, for nearly six weeks.

I took a look around Owen's apartment. I mean OUR apartment. It was a small one-bedroom with a million-dollar view (actually an $850,000 view, according to Mom, who said that's what Owen paid for this apartment, er, I mean condo, three years ago). I couldn't wait to tell Lily all about it. Living-room and dining-room windows looked out over Seattle's Elliott Bay and to Bainbridge Island. Even in the late spring there was some snow left on the peaks of the Olympic Mountains so that jagged white triangles towered beyond the water, making a backdrop that seemed almost fake because it was so postcard perfect. I headed out on the balcony and looked out at the water. I counted thirty-seven sailboats. A ferry belched its low horn, announcing it was on the move.

"That must be the Bainbridge Island ferry," Mom said. "We are going to have amazing sunsets. I think we're really going to like living here. Just look at all this!" She twirled around on the balcony and then leaned way over to look down. I felt like tossing my cookies.

"Um, where's the Space Needle?" I asked, trying to sound calm and perfectly at home on a tiny slab of concrete that jutted out nearly a hundred feet over the street.

"It's north and a bit behind us," Mom said. "You can't see it from here, not even if you lean way, waaaaay out." She swung her torso out and over the side. I shuddered. "Hmm . . .," Mom said. "I feel like I can see everything so clearly from here."

I opened my eyes and made sure she wasn't talking about my intense fear of heights. She was looking straight down to First Avenue, eleven stories below. I held on to the balcony railing, took a deep breath, and looked down. I gripped the railing even tighter. I felt a little dizzy. I stepped back, took another deep breath, and tried again. Nothing too remarkable, from my trying-not-to-barf-or-fall-off-the-balcony perspective. Just people walking on the sidewalks, a few people on bikes, and then a blur of purple and black as someone on a bike ripped around the corner and almost rammed into a jogger.

"That drives me crazy. Fast cyclists shouldn't be on the sidewalk, especially not someone from Swifty's," Mom said, heading back inside.

"Uh-huh," I replied. I had no idea what she meant, other than that speed-demon cyclists should ride on the street. I peered over the balcony railing again, just to prove I could. The purple-and-black-clad cyclist slowed down directly below us, hopping off his bike before he came to a stop. The large, flat package sticking out of the messenger bag that he had slung loosely across his back must have thrown him off balance a little, because his bike toppled to the curb against a parking meter. He didn't stop to pick up his bike or to lock it. It was like he was in perpetual motion. I had to stop looking down, or I'd be in perpetual throw-up mode. I settled into a deck chair on the balcony and refocused my energy on drawing the Olympic Mountains.

Sirens whined off in the distance. Then the sound got louder and louder, but I tried—unsuccessfully—to tune them out.

"Of course, we're going to have to get used to all the noise of living downtown." Mom came back out onto the balcony.

"It seems like they're coming right toward us," I said. I stood at the balcony's edge and dared myself to look down. A police car pulled up in front of Belltown Towers, and two uniformed officers got out. Another police car double-parked next to it, and then a solid blue car with a red light on top pulled in right behind the first one.

"What the heck is going on?" Mom asked.

"I don't know, but I'm going to find out," I said.

"Hannah, please don't get in their way," Mom said, following me out the apartment and down the hallway.

"I won't if you won't," I said. I stopped in front of the

elevator and watched the numbers above the doors. Each floor number lit up as the elevator passed it: 7, 8 . . . the elevator was heading toward our floor and then right past it . . . 11, 12. Then it stopped at *PH*.

Chapter 3

"Something must be wrong at the penthouse," I called to Mom.

"We can take the emergency stairs at the end of the hall," Mom said. She tries to be the rational adult, but she's just as nosy as I am.

I raced toward the door that said EXIT in glowing green letters. I bounded up the stairs, two steps at a time, counting each landing as I went. If we were on eleven, the penthouse apartments were just two flights up. "Twelve . . . thirteen," I said out loud. There was an unmarked door at the landing, but there was still another flight of stairs.

"I thought thirteen was the top floor."

"Let's try that door," Mom said, right at the heels of my purple high-tops. "I bet that last flight goes up to a roof garden or something."

I hurled the steel fire door open and was ready to bolt down the hall, but I stopped myself. It seemed like I'd entered a new world. Or at least a new building. Let me tell you, this top-floor hallway was nothing like the white-walled, blue-carpeted hallway down on eleven. Deep-piled, cushy carpet in a hunter green ran the length of the hallway, with a skinny red-and-gold plush Persian rug on top. The walls were painted a golden yellow orange, with gleaming dark wood trim. Oil paintings of landscapes and stuffy old-fashioned people hung on the walls in thick, ornate gold frames. I felt like I'd stepped into the den of an English lord's manor.

I shook myself out of my momentary awe and remembered why I'd raced up the stairs.

"Dorothy!" Mom rushed past me and toward heavy wood French doors that had PH-I and D. POWERS etched onto a gold oval nameplate. A uniformed police officer at the door put a hand up as if to say *Halt*. So we did. Dorothy came to the doorway, her facing looking paler and older than it had just a half hour earlier.

"Maggie, Hannah, please come in," she said. "It will be good to have some friends for support right now."

The police officer stepped aside and mumbled, "Go on in," to us.

Mom grabbed Dorothy's hand and walked her to a chair at the kitchen table. My mom is one of those people who can make anyone feel at ease, even during a crisis. Personally, I think she's a bit neurotic, but the rest of the world seems to find her amazingly calming.

I wasn't sure what to do. Follow Mom inside? Wait? Swap stories with the cop at the door? I stalled for time by looking down the corridor and checking out the scene. Right across the hall from ph-1 was its mirror image of double doors and a gold nameplate. Only this one said PH-II and M. CHOMSKY on the gold nameplate. The door to PH-2 opened a crack, then quickly closed. Weird. Did someone know that I was watching? Or did I know that someone was watching? I decided to head into Dorothy's kitchen.

"I'm fine, Maggie. Really. But I did have quite a scare," Dorothy said.

"What happened?" I blurted out. Mom gave me a quick glare. *What?* I mouthed back to her. I mean, I can't be expected to be the most patient person in the world when a crime has just been committed. I have a high need to know EVERYTHING. Okay, so no one actually said there'd been a crime. But why else would three cars with sirens and lights be parked in front of Belltown Towers?

Dorothy looked up and smiled wanly at me, then turned her attention back to my mother. "The odd thing is that it seemed like Ruff knew something was wrong," she said. "I've never seen him react to any delivery person that way before."

"Delivery? What delivery?" I asked. Mom glared at me again. I wanted to put a fast-forward on this scene and find out what happened.

"It was like any other delivery, except for the way that Ruff was acting," Dorothy went on. "I'm sure the Swifty's messenger had no idea what he was delivering." She stopped to take a sip of water.

What was he delivering? I wanted to blurt out, but I held it inside of me.

"This must have been quite the surprise, then," Mom said. She was looking across the table to what at first glance looked like a framed painting. I did a double take. The canvas was blank.

"That's so weird," I said, avoiding Mom's glare. Geesh. How many times could Mom glare at me in five minutes?

"What does it mean?" I asked Dorothy, ignoring my mother's nonverbal admonishments.

"I have no idea," she said. "All I know is that when Ruff and I got back from our walk, there was a voicemail message from Mimi Hansen saying she had a Swifty's bike messenger bringing me the painting I'd commissioned for the Honcho auction. No sooner had I heard her message than there was a knock on my door. I answered it thinking it might be you, Hannah, ready to take Ruff for a walk already."

"Someone knocked on your door? Isn't this a secure building, with an intercom and everything?" I asked.

"I'm not sure how the messenger got in, but that's not important," she said.

"I didn't know bike messengers worked on Sundays," Mom said.

"Oh, bike messengers work all kinds of hours," Dorothy

said. "I run into them all the time making deliveries right across the hall."

"So, what happened to the painting that was supposed to be delivered to you?" I asked, trying to get this conversation back on track.

"It must have been stolen, although we don't know where or when," Dorothy said. "That's why I called the police."

"Um, Ms. Powers?" a police officer asked, as if on cue. "We have almost everything we need, but we'll need to interview your neighbor, a Mister . . ."

"Mr. Chomsky," Dorothy said. "Marvin Chomsky."

"Yes, Mr. Chomsky was the one who called it in," the officer said.

"I asked him to call. I was so shaken up when I un-wrapped my painting. I was thrilled to finally have the new Hansen in my hands, but then I found this!" Dorothy said, gesturing toward the nonpainting. "But I doubt Mr. Chomsky can tell you anything. He never leaves his apartment. Messenger services bring him everything he needs."

"There's something else, Ms. Powers, if you don't mind," the officer continued. "Your dog. He seems to be in some sort of distress."

"Ruff? Distress? What's wrong?" I demanded.

"Perhaps I shouldn't have said 'distress,'" the officer said, a bit flustered. "He's under the bed and I can't coax him out."

"My reaction must have terrified him, especially once all the police arrived. Hannah, dear." Dorothy turned to me. "Would you go with Officer . . ."

"Officer Romano, ma'am," she said.

"Would you go with Officer Romano and see if you could bring Ruff out here? I think he'll come to you," Dorothy said. "Especially with this." She reached into her jacket pocket and gave me a little dog biscuit. "Dried liver," she whispered. "Just in case he needs added incentive."

I followed Officer Romano down a hallway.

"The dog's this way," Officer Romano said. "Did you say your name was Hannah?"

"Yes. I'm Ruff's dog walker," I said, trying to sound responsible. I didn't want to admit that I'd met the pooch less than an hour ago. "So, what kind of MO do you have on this case?" I asked. That's *modus operandi* in cop talk. I was a bit impressed with how effortlessly I rattled it off, especially since it's Latin. Roughly translated, it means "mode of operation," referring in criminal situations to how a perpetrator works.

"It's definitely not a standard case. And not just a prank, either. The substitute canvas suggests that someone knew exactly what was supposed to be in that package. Someone somewhere in this city has a valuable painting in their possession that they don't deserve to have," Officer Romano said.

"You've got to wonder how someone would have known

what was being delivered to Dorothy, though," I said. I didn't pursue it because we were in the bedroom.

At least I think it was a bedroom. There was a large bed (my first clue), but there was also a sitting area with a table and stacks of books. Another part of the room had a yoga mat, a big blue exercise ball, and a bar for stretching.

I could hear Ruff whimpering under the bed. I crouched down to look. He started to growl, but then he relaxed.

"Hey, Ruff. Come here, little guy," I cooed. Nothing. I pulled out the liver treat and reached far under the bed to wave it as enticement. Ruff bolted toward me (or toward the liver), dragging his leash along the wood floor until he nipped the liver right off my open palm. I scooped up the little terrier. He was trembling like he was cold or scared— or both. I sat down on the floor and cradled him in my arms. "It's going to be okay, little guy. I'll stick with you," I said as I petted him. He seemed to relax in my arms. I set him on the ground, but he started to whimper as soon as I let go of him. "So it's going to be that way, is it? You want me to carry you?" I scooped Ruff up into my arms again. "This is Ruff," I said to Officer Romano. She gave him a scratch behind the ears. I had a good feeling about this cop, a feeling that was confirmed when I felt Ruff relax even more. "I'd better get him back to his human," I said, heading out to the hallway.

". . . no one but Mimi Hansen knew just how valuable this painting was," Dorothy was saying to my mom.

"Why would she let something so valuable out of her sight, then?" I prodded.

"Hannah . . ." My mom seemed to be warning me. Hey, we needed to keep Dorothy talking while details were still fresh, right?

Officer Romano tried to fight off a smile.

"Does this count as a burglary or a robbery?" I asked her. "I mean, I know it's a burglary if no one is there. And it's a robbery if people are on the premises when something is stolen. So, since we can't know exactly when the real painting was stolen, would you officially call this a robbery or a burglary? OUCH!" I cried as Mom reached out with her foot and kicked me.

"We haven't released an official statement from the Seattle Police Department yet, but I think we're safe to call this an art theft," Officer Romano said.

"Right. It's a definite theft. Maybe even a heist," I offered.

Mom grimaced. "Hannah," she said, with more than just a smidgen of warning in her voice. It was sort of like she was saying "Don't be so dramatic." If she were an icky mom on a TV show, she would have said something like "You read too much" or "No more Crime Network for you."

Officer Romano had gone out into the main hallway for a phone call. She came back and looked extremely serious. "I need to tell you that there was a theft at the Mafune Gallery around the corner yesterday," she told Dorothy. "I'm not saying that the two cases are connected, but I thought you should know before the newspapers get ahold of this, since paintings by this same artist . . ." Officer Romano flipped through her notebook. "Yes, since both paintings were by this Mimi Hansen, I'm sure the media will blow this all out of proportion."

"Oh dear," Dorothy said. "Why on earth would someone target Mimi Hansen?"

Then she collapsed.

CHAPTER 4

I TOOK RUFF downstairs and outside. He had totally freaked out when Dorothy collapsed, and he started barking like crazy. I held Ruff while Mom helped Dorothy until we knew she was okay. She'd blacked out, something she said happens every once in a while because of some kind of blood-pressure something or other. I wasn't really paying attention. My mind buzzed with thoughts of this strange art heist. I had lots more questions, but the adults had dismissed me and the dog to another walk.

The police had already interviewed Dorothy before Mom and I got up to the penthouse, but clearly I'd brought up some excellent points. Then Officer Romano told me my services could be put to better use if I did my job as a dog walker.

The important thing was that Dorothy was okay. And that Ruff got some time outside.

Click, click, click.

I heard a clicking sound on the sidewalk. It sounded like someone was wearing baseball cleats and walking really fast. Almost like a horse trotting.

"Come on, boy, let's go this way," I said, leading Ruff around a corner.

Wham! All of a sudden I was on the ground. And someone or something had plowed into me. But what? I looked up.

"Watch where you're going!" I snapped from my sprawled position on the sidewalk. Ruff was squished under my right leg.

"Are you okay?" A guy in his twenties in full cycling gear—helmet, gloves, Lycra bike shorts—was looking down at me. He held out a hand to help me up. Ruff started to growl, but then stopped.

"If you move that fast without a bike, I'd hate to run into you when you were on a bike. . . ." I said, standing up and brushing off the seat of my shorts.

My voice trailed off. Mr. Bike Guy did a one-eighty and headed back the way he came before I could finish talking.

Click, click, click.

So that's what was making that noise. Bike Guy had those kind of cycling shoes that snap right into bike pedals. Lily's dad said they were great for riding a bike, but totally obnoxious and awkward when it came to trying to walk without looking like a dork. Bike Guy looked a little dorky as he sped up into race-walking mode. He darted around the corner at Battery Street, but not before I read the word *Swifty's* on his purple-and-black T-shirt.

"That was weird," I said to Ruff. Weird that Mom had just

said something about Swifty's. And definitely weird that in my first hour in my new neighborhood I'd already got up close and personal with the concrete.

A car horn honked. I leaped back from the curb, pulling Ruff with me. I didn't need to add a car accident to my list of mishaps today. A little white convertible pulled up to the curb right in front of Belltown Towers. A woman with blond hair and big dark incognito movie-star sunglasses jumped out and ran to the front of the building. She pressed one of the buttons that calls up to the apartments.

"Officer Romano," I heard over the intercom.

She must be calling the penthouse. I moved a little closer.

"I'm here to see Dorothy Powers," the woman said. She spoke as if the police officer upstairs were a maid. And how come she didn't wonder why a cop had answered the intercom? Maybe this woman was an investigator. She sure didn't look the part, but maybe she was working undercover or something.

"Your name, please?" Officer Romano's voice cackled over the intercom.

The woman sighed a bit impatiently. "Mimi Hansen," she announced.

Mimi Hansen! Wow. She didn't look at all how I expected an artist to look. She looked more like a TV talk-show host or something. She wore a short leopard-print skirt and a tight button jacket that matched it. On top of her head was a leopard-print hat, kind of like a beret you'd wear on Halloween if you were pretending to be a French artist. Her feet were strapped into the highest-heeled and pointiest-toed shoes I'd ever seen. Aren't artists supposed to look funky and poor, even if they aren't poor? Not this one. That's for sure.

I heard some garbled noise coming back over the intercom, and then the front door buzzed open. "Hold the door, please!" I called, pulling Ruff with me as I high-tailed it toward the open door. Mimi Hansen looked me up and down, stopping at my bony knees that were now scuffed up thanks to my run-in with the sidewalk. No matter what she thought of me and my bare legs, she still let me in. Sometimes being a kid has its advantages.

I smiled my most innocent smile.

"Hi. I'm just taking Ruff back up to his owner. You know, Dorothy Powers," I said.

"Oh, right. I thought that mutt looked familiar," she said, pushing the elevator "up" button.

Mutt?

"Actually, Ruff is a cairn terrier. A purebred. Not a mutt," I said importantly. I don't know why I felt I had to talk to her. There's just something so uncomfortable about standing around waiting for an elevator with someone.

"Of course it is," she said. She started jabbing the "up" button again, as if that would make the elevator come any faster.

Ruff crouched down. A low little growl came out of him.

She reached down to pet him. "Muff and I are old friends, aren't we, Muff?" she said.

Muff?

Ruff sprang up and started yipping. He jumped from side to side. He crouched down and growled again. Then he nipped at her hand.

"What's with that dog? Get it away from me!" she screamed.

The elevator doors opened. Ruff jumped inside and assumed his tough-guy crouch-and-growl position again. Mimi took a hesitant step forward. Ruff's growl got louder.

"You go on ahead," she said as she backed up. "I think I left something in the car." She cleared her throat. "Tell Dorothy that Mimi Hansen is on her way." It sounded like an order. Geesh. How many times did this woman need to announce herself?

CHAPTER 5

"IS EVERY DAY at Belltown Towers this eventuful, puppy?" Ruff didn't answer me, but he seemed to be settling down again. By the time the elevator reached the penthouse floor, Ruff was full of sloppy kisses and contented tail wags.

Dorothy and Mom were still sitting at the kitchen table.

"I think we're done for the day, Ms. Powers," Officer Romano said. "Please call us directly if you hear or see anything suspicious. Or if you think of anyone who might have wanted to do something like this to you."

"Oh, I'm supposed to tell you that Mimi Hansen is on her way here," I said. Mom looked at me curiously. "What?" I said to Mom. "I met her downstairs." I'm not sure, but I think my mom looked slightly impressed that I'd already met this artist person. I decided not to add that she'd been bossing me around.

"Oh, thank you, Hannah. And thank you, Officer Romano, for being so kind," Dorothy said.

"I hope you can relax with your guests now," Officer

Romano said. "I'll certainly keep you informed as we investigate your case." She bent down to scratch Ruff behind his ears. He licked her hand happily. She was just out the door when a human whirlwind made her entrance.

"Oh, Dorothy! I was so worried about you! Are you all right, darling?" Mimi Hansen rushed into the apartment, teetering on her ridiculously high-heeled shoes. She said "darling" so it sounded like "dahling."

Ruff started growling again.

"I'm fine, Mimi. But someone stole your painting on its way here!"

"What?" Mimi gasped.

"It's true. I'm just so sick about it. I was so excited to see *The Blue Principle* again before the Honcho auction, but when I opened the package, I saw this . . . this . . . this . . ." Dorothy gestured toward the empty canvas.

"What?" Mimi practically shrieked. She appeared to have an extremely limited vocabulary.

"Weird, huh?" I interjected. "You've got to wonder how someone even knew what was inside the package, since it was wrapped in plain brown paper and all."

"No one even knows about that painting but you and me," Mimi said, speaking directly to Dorothy, as if I hadn't uttered a word. "Why would someone target it?"

"It seems this thief has a good eye," Dorothy said.

"Yes, I see your point," Mimi said, suddenly composed. "That particular painting is exquisite in its play of light. It is a fine example of the quality of my work. Your thief has impeccable taste." She actually tried to chuckle. It didn't work.

"Yeah, but how did the thief know what painting was inside the package?" I said. "The switch must have been made before the bike messenger picked it up to bring over to Dorothy."

"I believe my young friend Hannah is correct," Dorothy said. "Oh! Forgive my bad manners! Mimi, these are my new neighbors, Maggie West and her delightful daughter, Hannah West. Maggie and Hannah, this is Mimi Hansen, one of the most promising artists on the West Coast."

"I've heard so much about your work," Mom said, holding out her hand. Mimi hesitated and then extended her hand for a limp nanosecond handshake. It seemed she was about to dismiss us when Mom added, "I write for *Art Voice*."

Mimi turned on a high-beam smile for Mom. At least I think it was a smile. The corners of her mouth were turned up, but it didn't reach the rest of her face. "Maggie, perhaps you already know that Dorothy is donating one of my creations to the Honcho auction. What you might not know yet is that Dorothy's generous spirit inspired me to create a second piece for the auction, the painting that was stolen. It's called *The Blue Principle*. It's part of a series I'm doing. One of the other pieces, *Principally Blue*, is right there," Mimi said, gesturing like a game-show model toward a big blue painting hanging on Dorothy's dining-room wall. I hadn't paid much attention before, but now it drew me into its swirls of blue. It was a painting of nothing, and a painting of everything. I stared at it. I felt like I could fly and swim at the same time. It truly was beautiful. Extraordinary, really.

"I didn't realize that was yours, Mimi," Mom said. "I didn't see your signature on it."

"I haven't signed it yet," Mimi murmured.

"I thought artists signed their work as soon as they finished," I piped up.

"Not always," Mimi said quickly, with a pointed glare toward me. At least she'd acknowledged that I was in the room.

"That's one of the many things that makes both *Principally Blue* and *The Blue Principle* so special!" Dorothy said. "It's such a clever idea that Mimi had for the Honcho auction."

"What's Honcho?" I asked, having heard about this auction twice in just the past few seconds.

"It's an auction that raises money for the arts in Seattle," Mom said. "Many arts groups couldn't survive without money from the Honcho auction."

"Exactly!" Dorothy said. "It was such a surprise when *Principally Blue* was delivered to my apartment. After I'd admired it for a few minutes, I noticed it didn't have that characteristic Mimi Hansen signature that she's so well known for. I thought that was puzzling, so I called Mimi right away."

Mimi shifted in her chair. She recrossed her legs. I flinched reflexively, afraid that one of those high-heeled shoes would spear me.

"Mimi pretended it was an oversight at first." Dorothy laughed. "As if she would actually forget to put her signature on a painting like this."

"Well, I can get forgetful while in the throes of my creative energy, you know. . . ." Mimi trailed off.

"That's when Mimi told me her big surprise! She hadn't signed it on purpose. That way, we can create excitement at the auction because Mimi will be there to sign this painting in front of a crowd of some of the wealthiest people in the city."

"How unusual," Mom muttered.

"It's actually quite a brilliant idea I had," Mimi said, attempting once again to chuckle. It sounded more like an evil vampire's laugh. "In fact, it was such a good idea that I decided to create the other painting. Of course, I didn't sign that one, either."

"Maybe that's why someone wanted to steal it," I said.

"Because the thief didn't want the auction to make money?" Dorothy asked.

"Because of my brilliant idea?" Mimi asked.

"No. Because if it didn't have a signature, how could you prove it was a Mimi Hansen? If it's such a good painting, and I'm sure it is," I hurriedly added, "then someone else could take credit for it and sell it."

Dorothy and Mom stared at me.

Ruff licked my hand.

Mimi glared at me again. She was getting good at it.

CHAPTER 6

BY TWO O'CLOCK on Sunday, I'd moved into a new apartment, got a job as a dog walker, met a famous artist, almost witnessed an art heist, and started a new investigation. I was hungry.

I grabbed my sketch pad, and Mom and I headed out to explore our temporary neighborhood. Belltown is part of downtown Seattle, but it's just north of the big businesses and tall glass skyscrapers. Condos, coffee shops, restaurants, bakeries, coffee shops, apartments, art galleries, coffee shops, and bars line the streets of Belltown. Did I mention coffee shops? Seattle is a bit coffee crazed, and it's not just because Starbucks HQ is here. Anyway, Belltown is the kind of neighborhood where you can eat your way around the world, with Japanese, Cuban, Vietnamese, Spanish, Chinese, Greek, Mexican, Italian, and French restaurants—but no fast-food joints—all within an easy walk.

"Is there some kind of zoning law here? Like, 'There must be one art gallery, one restaurant from each continent, and two coffee shops per city block,'" I said.

"Make that each side of the street for each block, and I think you've summarized Belltown pretty well," Mom said. "So, what will it be, the Noodle Ranch or the Noodle House?" We were right in front of the Noodle Ranch, and we would have had to go all the way across the street to get to the other Thai noodle restaurant. The Noodle Ranch it was.

When you're technically homeless and your mom is a waitress, spending money at restaurants isn't exactly high on the list of things to do. I never knew noodles could taste as good as they did at the Noodle Ranch. And talk about affordable! I suggested doing a taste test and heading to the Noodle House for dinner, but Mom said we still needed to watch our budget. "Besides, there's lots to do back at our apartment," she added.

It feels weird to call it "our" apartment because it's really Owen's. That night I curled up on Owen's eggplant-colored leather couch and looked over the sketches I'd started earlier that day. I'm what's known in my family as an OCS (obsessive-compulsive sketcher), which Mom says is an artistically accepted cousin to OCD (obsessive-compulsive disorder). She also says it might work well with my crime investigation, since OCD doesn't deter San Francisco detective Adrian Monk on the TV show *Monk*. He can't pass a lamppost without touching it. I can't pass a lamppost without sketching it. Compulsive sketching pays off, though. I have lots of material to shape into my newest graphic novel venture, starring a brilliant young girl of Chinese descent on the trail of a mysterious art thief.

"Hannah," Mom interrupted me from my drawing state. "I just got a call from Wired." She sat down on the couch next to me, clutching her cup of herbal tea. I could smell Monkey Jasmine. Mom may work at a coffee shop called Wired Café, but she never drinks coffee. Just tea. "I can do an extra shift tomorrow, but I'll need to be there by five-thirty."

"In the morning?" I whined.

"Yep. I'm really sorry, but you know we—"

"—need the money," I finished for her.

She hugged me, spending a little extra time, like she was going to say more. Then efficient Mom Mode took over, and she spread out three Metro bus schedules on the coffee table. "I think you know all the north-end routes, but here are schedules for the 72, 42, and 7."

Mom went over my bus options while I tried to turn off the continuous recording in my head: *I hate being homeless . . . I hate being homeless . . . I hate being homeless . . .*

I know, I know, I know: I'm not truly homeless. Technically homeless, yes. But out on the streets? No. Sleeping in a car? No. Living under a bridge? No. And yet it's so close.

Every once in a while I like to have a little pity party with yours truly as the guest of honor. That's what I did our first night in Belltown Towers. Not even a million-dollar view (or an $850,000 view, in this case) could get me past feeling sorry for myself. But cable TV is the perfect guest at the Hannah West Pity Party.

I put my sketch pad away and started flipping channels. Total score. Owen had more cable channels than our last house-sitting job had offered. I flipped quickly from Channel 2 all the way into the eighties. "Come on, come on . . . Yes!" Channel 85 was TCN, The Crime Network, twenty-four hours of crime right in your home. I loved this channel. The Crime Network had the real-life investigative shows with detectives and scientists. It also had lots of police dramas like *CSI* and *Law & Order*, funny ones like *Monk*, plus super old detective shows like *Columbo*.

"Now, this is educational television," I said, settling in to rewatch the end of a *Monk* episode. Aside from building my logic and deduction skills, my crime-TV watching keeps my math skills sharp. According to my calculations, I currently have a 92 percent success rate solving crimes. On television, that is.

I watched another episode of *Monk*, one that I hadn't seen yet, and actually forgot to keep feeling sorry for myself.

Nothing like solving a mystery to cheer me right up.

Hannah West's TV Crime Solving Success Rate: 94 percent.

CHAPTER 7

"GET UP AND SHAKE YOUR BOOTY! SHAKE YOUR BOOTY!"

Ever notice how hard it is to get up on a Monday morning? That's why I, Hannah J. West, employ a little obnoxious disco helper.

"I said: GET UP and shake your booty!" I hit the "snooze" button on my disco alarm. I knew I'd pay for it later.

Five minutes later: *"Did you not hear me? I said: GET UP AND SHAKE YOUR BOOTY!"* The disco queen was louder and screechier, accompanied by a mini-disco light show and rotating silver mirrored ball. I've really got to move that thing across the room so that I absolutely have to get out of bed the first time it tells me to shake my booty. Especially when it's my first day in a new place and my mom is already at work.

I hit the street at 7:20, heading to Third and Pine to catch the number 72 bus. Perfect timing.

Mom was right. I really was a pro at this. Ever since I was little, she and I had gone all over the city of Seattle on Metrobuses, from the Alki lighthouse in West Seattle (number 66 downtown, then transfer to the number 56 or 37; total trip time fifty-two minutes from our old house) to the swimming beaches at Lake Washington (number 2 from downtown for twenty-one minutes), and just about everywhere in between. She didn't let me go by myself until sixth grade, and even then she made absolutely sure that I knew what I was doing. I did. Of course. And now it was totally worth it. Being able to get around the city on Metro meant I could keep going to Cesar Chavez Middle School, no matter where we were house-sitting.

I got off six blocks from school. I didn't want any snoopy or snooty parents to see me on a city bus. No matter how bad middle school can be, at least Chavez isn't completely miserable. It's the north end's AA school. Officially, that's for "Alternative and Accelerated." Everyone at Chavez is considered "advanced." Whatever *that* means. You have to have certain test scores or recommendations from teachers to go there. You also had to live north of the Ship Canal. We used our old address in the Maple Leaf neighborhood for my school assignment. We were superlucky there, too, because the people renting our old house kept our mail for us.

I was a block from Chavez Middle when a little white two-seater convertible with a BMW emblem screeched past me and pulled over to the curb. I had a flashback to Mimi Hansen parking in front of Belltown Towers yesterday. Uh-oh. It *was* Mimi Hansen. But she wasn't getting out here. A blond girl about my age stepped out of the passenger side. The door hadn't even closed all the way when Mimi accelerated away.

The girl looked around, as if checking out who was watching her. She glanced at me, then looked quickly away. She was the kind of girl who *wanted* to be watched (especially getting a ride to school in a spiffy car like that). But she also looked nervous, as if she *didn't* want anyone to see her. She was heading toward the front doors of Chavez, just like I was. She turned around and glared at me again, as if I were following her. Well, I was, technically. But only because I had to get to school before the final bell. If she was starting at Chavez, the New Girl Alert would spring into action, and we'd know all about her by lunchtime. This girl was one mystery I didn't have time for.

The first bell rang, and I headed into school and straight for homeroom.

"Hey," I said to Lily.

"Hey back," she said. She didn't even look up from her book, but she wasn't being rude. She was just being Lily. And that means preoccupied with a story. She unclipped her bangs on the right side and reclipped them, then did the same thing on the left side, managing to turn a page in the middle of clipping. Both of us play with our hair—I'm a hair twirler and she's a hair twister—and both of us are trying to get out of the habit. Today Lily had her shoulder-length straight brown hair in two pigtails twisted into buns. She says if she restricts her hair she won't play with it as much. The result is that my fair-skinned, blue-eyed, freckled Irish friend looks like a cross between a leprechaun and Princess Leia from the original *Star Wars* movies. But I'm not about to tell her that. Her right hand reached up for her hair clip.

"Put the clip down," I whispered in a mock-cop voice. "Walk away from the clip and we'll all be okay."

She looked up at me. Glared up at me, actually. Then back to her book.

"Who done it?" I asked, flopping my messenger bag down next to her desk.

"Not sure yet," she replied, still not looking up. Lily was on an Agatha Christie mystery binge. She'd gone on a mystery-reading jag last summer, starting with Sir Arthur Conan Doyle and then moving on to Dame Agatha. She was on a mission to read every single book by Agatha Christie.

I peeked at the cover of her book: *Murder at the Vicarage*.

"What's a vicarage, and who was murdered there?" I asked.

Lily still didn't look up. "A vicarage is like a church. I don't yet know who murdered the magistrate. I daresay it wasn't the vicar, but I'm not sure I trust Griselda. However, I do believe it was someone in the parish."

"Huh?"

"Hannah, you really need to learn to speak British if

you want to keep up with me, old chum," Lily said with a bloody good accent. "Now leave me alone so I can get to the bottom of this before Miss Marple."

"Don't forget our local art-thief mystery, Miss Shannon," I said. Lily and I had e-mailed back and forth yesterday, so she was up on the action at Belltown Towers.

"Listen up, people," Mr. Claussen, our homeroom teacher, called. "We've got a few announcements, and then we'll take the rest of the period for quiet time. You can read, do homework, sleep, or draw." He looked right at me at the end, which I assume was for the drawing suggestion, as I'm not much of a classroom sleeper.

"It's so unfair," I whispered to Lily. "An entire school year will go by without us having a class together, and we don't even get to talk in homeroom half the time." The cruel scheduling program didn't even give Lily and me the same lunch period.

She sighed dramatically and went back to Miss Marple, and I worked on a female sword-wielding manga bike messenger until the bell for second period rang.

"Note you?" I queried.

"Note me," Lily confirmed. "I'll note you back."

We were on a retro covert communication mission. Everyone at Chavez was into instant messaging after school and text messaging between classes. I'd read this article about students in Japan who were actually using paper and pencil to scribble notes to one another, then using their camera phones to take a picture, and sending the note to a friend. The whole idea was so preposterous that Lily and I vowed to be devoted paper-note correspondents.

We headed out the door. I raced down two flights of stairs and along a long hallway to the art studio. The one good thing about my schedule this year was that I'd finally gotten into Drawing/Painting 3. Getting to draw first thing in the morning was some consolation for not having the same lunch as Lily. I sat down at my regular table and got out my colored pencils. I am totally in love with the Prismacolor pencils my grandma gave me for my last birthday. They're not at all like the ordinary colored pencils you get at the drugstore or Office Warehouse. These are considered "artist quality," with wonderful pigment. It's easier to control your color and line with really good pencils. And thanks to Grandma, I had a deluxe box of 120.

"Let's get started," Ms. Murdoch said. She expected us to be ready to work as soon as the final bell rang.

"You can sit right there by Hannah," Ms. Murdoch said. I hadn't been paying attention until she said my name.

I looked up as that new blond girl sat down next to me at the table. I smiled. She didn't.

"This will be your permanent seat for the rest of the quarter," Ms. Murdoch told her.

Great, I thought. This girl didn't seem terribly friendly. Besides, I'd gotten used to having the whole table to myself.

The new girl smiled at Ms. Murdoch. Then she mumbled, "Just great."

At least I hadn't said anything out loud. Or had I?

"Um, I'm Hannah," I said.

"I'm Jordan," she said.

"Where are you from?"

"Bellevue," she answered. And that one word said it all. Bellevue is a suburb on the other side of Lake Washington. Superrich people live in Bellevue, including Bill Gates, one of the guys who started Microsoft—who, in case you haven't heard, is the richest person in the world.

"I want you to start right away sketching this still life. Don't worry about colors or details at this point, of course," Ms. Murdoch said, looking at me since I already had my colored pencils out. "Concentrate on the forms and their relational sizes." It was an odd assortment of things for a still life—a small African-style drum, a clay vase with a single tulip, and an old-lady kind of teacup and saucer with dainty pink roses around the rims. The combination did not look particularly intriguing or attractive. I wasn't sure if there was some weird hidden symbolism in these objects.

"I hope we don't have to talk symbolism," Jordan said under her breath.

I stifled a laugh. Maybe this new girl from the suburbs wasn't too bad after all.

"I like your highlights," she said. "They remind me of

Vermilion. Or maybe Carmine Red."

Interesting. This girl didn't say "red." She used specific Prismacolor pencil hues. Most people just say, "I like those reddish streaks in your hair."

"Actually, I think of this more as Crimson Lake," I said. "Number 925," I added, to see if she really knew her stuff. She smiled, so I guess she did. I was going to ask why she'd switched schools so close to the end of the year, but the teacher was heading toward us.

"Jordan, I'm so thrilled to have you in class," Ms. Murdoch said breathily. "I'm a huge fan of your mother's work. I couldn't believe it when I read in the *Times* this morning that someone stole one of her paintings from the Mafune Gallery and then another one en route to Belltown Towers."

I stared at Jordan. "Is your last name Hansen?" I asked.

"No, it's Walsh," she said.

"But Mimi Hansen—"

"—is my mother," Jordan finished for me. She had that steel-eyed look that said, *You want to make something of it?*

"Oh, wow. I just met her yesterday. She's really famous. I saw this painting she did called *Principally Blue*. It's gorgeous."

"Yeah, right. I'll bet it is. She's sure some artist." Jordan clearly wasn't interested in talking with me. Or maybe about her mom.

CHAPTER 8

THE BELL RANG. I packed up my things and headed toward the door. Jordan followed me out. I was still trying to get my head around all of a sudden having a new girl in school who just happens to be the great Mimi Hansen's daughter. But then I turned into Hannah West, Helpful Girl and Ambassador of Kindness to new students. "Do you need help finding your next class? I can give you the lowdown on the best lunch line, too," I offered.

"Are you both the school artist and tour guide?" Jordan asked. She said "artist" so it sounded like "artiste." Then she added, "By the way, where did you get your Prismacolor-inspired streaks?" She smiled while she talked and walked. At least, the corners of her mouth were turned up, but her face wasn't really going along with it. I suddenly saw the family resemblance between Jordan Walsh and Mimi Hansen. Twenty-four hours ago, I had never even heard of Mimi Hansen. Now she was everywhere, including a younger version right beside me in the halls of Chavez Middle.

I stopped and Jordan practically screeched to a stop beside me. Was she making fun of me and my hair? I'd have to cut ties with her now before she commented on my vintage Urban Surf T-shirt or managed to find something wrong with my jeans.

"Listen, Jordan, I'm not exactly sure why we're talking about Prismacolor names or my hair, but if there's something I can help you with at Chavez, let me know," I said.

"Ladies! Welcome!" Mr. Ogata came out in the hall. "Your presence is requested inside my fascinating class," he said. "We have a lot to go over today."

Jordan followed me into Mr. Ogata's room. Just my luck. Jordan Walsh was in social studies with me, too. And that meant she was an honors student.

I copied our homework assignment from the board, but I didn't hear a word Mr. Ogata said for fifty-five minutes. All my brain cells were fired up and fuming, but also swirling and muddled. How could someone I didn't even know act so weird around me? I tried to look like I was paying attention to Mr. Ogata, but I doubt I was very convincing.

Finally, social studies was over. But my time with Jordan Walsh wasn't. It dawned on me that if she was in social studies with me, she'd also be in honors language arts. Jordan got up to leave.

"Not so fast," Mr. Ogata said as he came over to her. "I'll

try not to be hurt that you're so eager to leave me. But this is a two-hour honors block. Check your schedule, Ms. Walsh, and if it says 'Honors Language Arts,' then you're staying here with the rest of these inquiring minds." Jordan made a show of pulling out her schedule and looking it over, then she gave a big sigh and settled back into her seat.

"You all have five minutes to talk softly, stretch, do some yoga or mental gymnastics," Mr. Ogata said. "And then I'll be introducing you to the wonderful Mary Wollstonecraft Shelley."

I used my five minutes to draw a retro note to Lily. I wasn't sure if the sports car, the glammed-up image of Mimi Hansen, and the doodles of Jordan in my first three classes of the day would mean much to Lily at this point, but it was fun to draw.

Jordan stayed in her seat across the aisle from me, but she left my mind within minutes of Mr. Ogata telling us about the world of a young girl named Mary Wollstonecraft, who, by the age of twenty, had written and published one of the most famous novels of all time. We had only thirty minutes left to start reading that novel, *Frankenstein*. I could barely stop when the bell rang for lunch.

I shoved my books into my locker, pulled out my sketch pad, and headed to the lunchroom. I got a bean burrito, carrots, and chocolate milk from the lunch line. I get free hot lunch, thanks to Mom's low-wage job. I've read in some books that getting hot lunch is a sure sign that you're poor. It's not that way at Chavez Middle School at all. You get to pick from three main things every day—like pizza, burritos, taquitos—and usually one of the choices is decent. You "pay" by punching in your secret code. No one knows whether you used a hundred-dollar bill, your dad's American Express card, or a free pass to pay for your food.

Even all the TC girls (The Clique girls) buy hot lunch. It's too much of a hassle to bring a lunch. Chavez Middle is a "model environmental school." If you bring your lunch, every container you bring has to be reusable. No brown bags that get tossed into the garbage. No Ziploc bags unless you plan to reuse them. And let's face it: We sixth graders don't have time to wash out our Ziploc bags. That would take away from the wonderful social lives we enjoy.

Yeah, right.

I sat on a stoop on the side stairs with my sketch pad. I needed to get Jordan Walsh and Mimi Hansen out of my head. So I put them on paper again.

By the time the bell rang for sixth period, Jordan had turned into Medusa. I must say, snakes growing out of her scalp looked eerily natural on her. I added it to my other pictograph note to Lily and added, "Guess who is in three of my classes?" and then folded the note into tight triangles until it was less than one inch big. On my way to sixth-period Japanese, I slipped my retro paper note through one of the slots in Lily's locker.

CHAPTER 9

"YO, HANNAH! Wait up!" Lily called to me.

I slowed a little but kept walking. "Hey, Lily."

"Why are you in such a hurry to get to the bus?" she panted.

"Just keep walking. I'm trying to avoid someone. I'll tell you later," I mumbled. "But keep talking and walking. Like we're having a fascinating conversation."

Lily did some loud fake laughter. "Oh, that is too funny! What did she do next?" That's my best friend. A born actress. I could count on her to switch into character at a split second's notice.

"Did you have to make it a *her*?" I grumbled. "I just hope she's not around."

Lily had no idea who or what I was talking about. But she didn't miss a beat. "You mean you saw your cousin and her boyfriend right in the middle . . ."

That got some looks from the kids around us. We were moving like a pack out to the bus lines.

"Okay, okay. Good job. You saved my face." I laughed back to Lily.

"Yeah, well, no problem. But when we get on the bus, you're telling all."

Getting on the bus is part of my daily charade of being Hannah Jade West, the middle-class girl who lives with her mother in their comfortable two-bedroom home in Seattle's Maple Leaf neighborhood.

In the winter, Mom wanted me home by 5:00 or 5:30 because it got dark so early. That meant getting off the school bus, picking up the mail at our old address, and heading back on Metro to wherever we were house-sitting. But now that it's almost summer, it stays light until eight o'clock or later at night. I could hang out with Lily until dinner and still make it the seven miles back downtown with plenty of daylight left.

Lily and I had planned to put on our sleuthing hats during the bus ride home, but first I needed help figuring out why Jordan had acted so strange to me.

"Do you think she got kicked out of her old school?" Lily asked.

"That seems pretty extreme," I said, mulling this over. "But it's definitely weird that she'd switch schools so close to the end of the school year."

"I'd throw a fit if my parents tried to get me to move to a new school right now," Lily said.

"Maybe she needed a clean start."

"She needs a code name," Lily said. "Got one?"

"Haven't thought of one yet," I said. "Let's see . . ." Lily and I have code names for practically everybody we ever need to talk about. That way we can talk freely—usually—about people. The trick is to find codes that aren't too predictable, but not so complicated that we can't remember them ourselves.

"JW or IJW for Icky Jordan Walsh." Lily started brainstorming.

"No obvious initials. I'd bet a hundred dollars that her friends call her 'J-Dub,'" I said. "That is, if she has any friends."

"Oh! I have it! Mini Mimi!" Lily started singing "me me me" scales, like an opera singer warming up. I joined in with "Mini me me me, Mini me me me" until we both collapsed in giggles.

"I. Have. An. Idea." Lily gasped, trying to stop laughing. "How about NJ, for Nasty Jordan? We don't actually know that she's nasty, but we've got some early indicators."

"Enj?" I tried sounding it out instead of using the initials. "Enj," I said again.

"Perfect! Easy to remember. Rolls right off my tongue."

We got off the bus on Northeast Eightieth Street and Eighth Avenue. Jamie, the bus driver, winked at me. Uh-oh. Did that wink mean Jamie knew I was just pretending to live up in Maple Leaf?

"Okay, Lily. Do you want to go to my house or your house?" I said loudly as I clambered off the bus.

"Can we go to mine first?" Lily said, just as loudly. Geesh, can you see why I love this girl? She's a true best friend. She should get an Academy Award for Best Actress Supporting Hannah West's Game of Deception.

If Jamie the bus driver was paying any attention to us, I thought we'd given pretty good cover.

We headed to Lily's house. First on the agenda: Stress Dancing. We turned up the stereo in her family room superloud and jumped around. After three songs, Lily turned down the stereo, and we headed for homework and cookies.

At five o'clock, Lily's dad and little brother, Zach, got home. I started getting my stuff together to leave.

"Can you stay for dinner, Hannah?" Lily's dad asked. "I'm experimenting with a new dish tonight. It's rich with antioxidants and fiber."

"Thanks, Dan, but I can't," I said hurriedly. I'd forgotten that Lily's dad was creating new recipes and writing a cookbook for his organic food co-op. His working title for the book was *Life Gets Better with Kale.* No matter how much I like the Shannons, I didn't feel like learning what kale was. "I'm going to head downtown and meet my mom. It's easy this time. We're staying at the Belltown Towers."

"Wow. Pretty fancy. Do you have a view?" Dan asked.

"Yep. Eleventh floor corner unit, full view. And it's all ours—at least for six weeks."

"It seems like I just read something about the Belltown Towers in the *Times* this morning," Dan said.

"News at the Belltown Towers? Let's see . . . robbery, art heist, and all kinds of high-end intrigue. We're in the thick of it," I said.

"The paper said the robber pulled a fast one, switching a blank canvas for an authentic Hansen painting that was about to be delivered to some wealthy art patron. That sounds like a smart villain. I love Hansen's work," Dan said.

"Really? You do? Why?" I really wanted to know. What was it about this artist that had everyone's eyes lighting up?

"Well, I guess I don't love all her stuff," Dan said. "Then again, that's what's so great about her. You can't peg her style. Almost every piece is different. She's got tremendous range."

"Range?"

"Some landscapes, some abstract, some soft and subdued," Dan said. "I could go on and on about it—"

"But you won't," Lily cut him off. "Because Hannah has to go. Right, Hannah?"

"Right." Thank you again, Lily Shannon. I'd decided that I'd had enough talk of Mimi Hansen for a while.

CHAPTER 10

I SPRINTED DOWN to Eightieth Street. Timing is everything.

And my timing is perfect—at least when it comes to Metro buses. It's like I have this weird mechanism inside that's perfectly tuned in to Seattle city buses. Sometimes I'll be sitting in class and I'll look at my watch and think, *Hmm . . . 1:32 P.M. The number 6 will be at Third and Pine right about now.* I have the schedules and routes memorized for sixteen different buses. Best yet, I always get to a bus stop right on time.

Like now. I got to the stop on Northeast Eightieth Street just as the 66 came into view. I hopped on and found a window seat for the ride downtown. Here's another little tip I've learned in my Metro riding experience: Always wear headphones. No one bothers you if you look like a kid listening to loud music. My mini-player was out of batteries. In fact, I didn't even have my mini with me. But with my earbuds in place, I pulled out my sketch pad and looked around for a victim . . . Er, I mean, I looked for a fellow passenger to draw.

I'll give him a try, I thought to myself. The guy sitting two rows ahead and across the aisle from me looked kind of familiar, in that brown-haired kind of cute older guy (midtwenties) kind of way. Too old for me and too young for my mom, but I had my eye on him for another reason. He had that five o'clock shadow thing going on. Drawing people is hard no matter what, but perfecting the shadowing needed for facial hair is an extra challenge. One of the characters in my graphic novel has two days' growth of beard. I needed to work on stubble. I decided to manga-ize this guy, drawing him Japanese comic style.

I got so engrossed in my drawing that the bus was all the way south of the Pike Place Market and the Seattle Art Museum before I noticed I'd missed my Stewart Street stop. Darn it. I pulled the cord to signal the bus driver someone wanted off at the next stop. I stuffed my sketch pad in my backpack and headed to the front of the bus.

The guy I'd been drawing hopped off ahead of me and took a bike off the bike rack in front. He started walking his bike down the street.

Click, click, click.

This time I recognized the sound. Bike cleats. The same sound I'd heard outside Belltown Towers yesterday. It made perfect sense that he'd make that noise. He had a bike, after all, not to mention black cycling shorts, a purple hooded sweatshirt, and one of those bike messenger bags slung across his chest.

Come to think of it, both the thief at Belltown Towers and Bike Guy had messenger bags like that. So, maybe the thief was a bike messenger? Okay, wait. I needed to remember that old phrase "Don't shoot the messenger." The bike messenger was just delivering a package. Someone had probably switched the bags before the messenger even started pedaling off on the delivery. Right?

Or was my imagination getting a little overactive?

Maybe not. The bike guy from the bus took off his sweatshirt. He was wearing a purple-and-black Swifty's bike-messenger jersey.

Maybe I wasn't so crazy after all.

I did what any normal twelve-year-old sleuth would do.

I pulled out my cell phone.

"Lily! Where are you?" I said to her answering machine. "Hannah here. I'm hot on the trail of a bike messenger. Could be the same one I saw outside Belltown Towers . . ."

Beep.

Lily picked up the phone.

"Do you have any idea how many bike messengers there are in Seattle?" she asked.

"No, but this one is wearing a Swifty's shirt. And so was the one at Belltown Towers. Are you going to tell me that's just a coincidence?"

"Do you have any idea how many bike messengers work

at Swifty's and wear those jerseys?" Lily asked.

"Well, how many of them ride the bus instead of a bike?"

"Maybe the ones who are riding the bus downtown to get to work," Lily offered in a patronizing voice, like she was explaining the absolute obvious to me. "Some of those Metro buses have bike racks in front. My dad and I put our bikes there when we took the bus to the Arboretum last summer."

"Stop with the logic and the family stories," I whined. "What if *this* guy is the art thief? Maybe he's working with the guy who knocked me over yesterday? Like his accomplice, or a lookout or something."

"Well, then, my paranoid little friend," Lily said slowly, "you might as well indulge yourself in your art-thief theory and follow the guy. Go ahead. Follow him!"

Of course, I was already following him while I talked on the phone. He was conveniently heading north, walking alongside his bike, heading in the same direction I needed to go to get home to Belltown Towers. When he leaped on his bike and started pedaling, I had to hold myself back. Just because there was a slim, slight, minuscule, teensy-tiny chance that the thief was a cyclist didn't mean that this cyclist was a thief. Lily was right. Downtown Seattle was teeming with cyclists. Bike messengers wove in and out of traffic on weekdays, not to mention all the people who commuted to their jobs on bikes.

Before I knew it, I had lost him.

I looked around for the nearest bus stop and realized that I was at Second and Pine, close to Nina's studio space. I might as well see if Nina was around. Nina, my mom's best friend, let me keep an easel and some supplies in a corner of the studio. She shared the studio space with a bunch of other artists, but she said I was welcome to work on my own stuff as long as she was there. I was so close, I decided not to call first. I'd stop by, like people are always doing in books and on TV shows.

When I got to First Avenue, I looked up at the fourth floor of the Stimson Building. Lights were on in Studio 4, Nina's studio space. I was about to buzz the studio when . . .

Click, click, click.

Man, was my mind destined to endless echoes of that clicking sound? It was getting to be like an annoying song that gets stuck in your head, like those high-pitched girls singing "Tell me more, tell me more" in that song from *Grease.* Only this time the cleats were thundering—and they were real—and they were coming down the stairs inside the building. The door swung open.

"Thanks, I was about to buzz," I said, catching the door, as the same bike guy from my bus came out. No time to exchange pleasantries, apparently. My hunch about him being a thief evaporated. He was just an ordinary Swifty's bike messenger, picking up an ordinary oversize package at the Stimson Building.

He jumped on his bike and took off remarkably fast. It

was remarkable because he was also carrying a large flat object wrapped in brown paper. Sort of like what I'd seen yesterday when I was on the eleventh-floor balcony at Belltown Towers.

CHAPTER 11

I GRABBED THE door to the Stimson before it closed so I could run up to the studio without buzzing. If Nina wasn't there, I could at least leave her a note. I sprinted two steps at a time to the fourth floor. The dimly lit hallway had five doors leading into what realtors advertised as "loft space for artists." Nina shared a space with a bunch of artists I'd never even met.

The door to Studio 4 was open a crack.

"Nina?" I called as I walked in.

Music came from a boom box in the corner, and I thought I heard water running in the back. Maybe Nina was there washing out brushes.

"Nina? It's me, Hannah," I called again.

A tall man with dreadlocks came out of the washroom.

"Yes? Nina is not here," he said. He had that kind of Jamaican/Rasta-sounding voice.

"Oh. Sorry," I said. "The door was open, so I thought I'd see if she was in here working. I'm a friend of hers."

The man didn't say anything.

"Nina lets me hang out here sometimes and do some work. That's my easel over there," I said, pointing to a corner.

He moved over in front of some paintings lined up against the wall. "Nina is not here," he said again.

I guess that should have been my cue to leave. But noooo. . . . Something caught my eye. My artist's eye, as Mom would say.

"Are these yours? These are fabulous," I said, walking toward the three small canvases behind this guy. Maybe I should have been on guard about being in a building with a total stranger. But he wasn't really a stranger if he worked with Nina. She and her studio mates were always supercareful about who they shared their space with. Besides, as I stared at the three paintings, I was getting pulled into a world of swirling blues. I couldn't look away. I stepped closer, and scenes of alleys and streets unfolded in the myriad of blues. Each painting was only about a foot wide, but it was full of details, giving it the impression of being much larger. "The play of light in this one is so intriguing," I said. Eww! I sounded like a hoity-toity art person. But the words *play of light* were jumping around in my mind. Where had I heard that phrase recently?

The man shuffled from foot to foot.

"Um, my name is Hannah West," I said. I held out my hand. "Like I said, I'm a friend of Nina Krimmel's. Actually, she and my mom, Maggie, are friends. She just tolerates me."

He shook my hand quickly and let go. "I am James," he said.

"I love your work. I feel like I've seen it before. . . ."

"It is not ready to be seen yet," he said.

"I guess that's why you haven't signed these three," I said.

"I do not mean to be rude to one of Nina's friends, but perhaps it is now time for you to leave," he said. Was it my imagination, or was James a little nervous? I know a lot of artists are perfectionists (a trait that hadn't appeared in me yet) and didn't want anyone to see their work until it was absolutely perfect. James's paintings looked pretty darn perfect to me.

"I'm sorry to have bothered you while you were working," I said. "Is it okay if I leave Nina a note?"

"Yes, yes. Leave her a note. And then I think you should go," he said.

I turned to a fresh sheet of paper in my sketch pad and did a rough sketch of one of James's blue street paintings. I hoped it looked like I was writing. James went back to the sink area. Then he came back and draped a paint-splattered sheet over the three paintings.

"These are not ready to be seen," James said yet again. "Come back some other time, when Nina is here." He went back to cleaning brushes.

I drew a superquick sketch of James. I left a note folded for Nina.

Nina,

I stopped by. Can I come paint some
night this week?

—H.W.

"Has your work been in a gallery?" I called out to James.
"I feel like I've seen it before."

I heard a woman's voice in the hallway.

". . . I'm at the Stimson Building to see what James
has ready to go. I need at least one more from him, plus
whatever we get at The Factory on Friday night. . . ."

It was one of those annoying cell yellers—the kind of
person who walks around with a cell phone constantly
glued to her head, talking loud. What's really annoying is
that you get only half the conversation—the cell yeller's
half—when you eavesdrop. It's terribly unsatisfying.

"The messenger is on his way. . . ." the cell yeller said,
but then her voice dropped and I couldn't hear. Something
about "making a witch" or "making a switch." Whatever.

The cell yeller was getting louder and the door to Studio
4 opened wider.

Mimi Hansen walked in.

CHAPTER 12

"WE'LL TALK LATER," Mimi said into her phone. She flipped it shut with a snap.

"James, I thought you'd be alone. I thought we had an understanding that your work was highly secretive," Mimi said. She glared at me, even though she was talking to James, with absolutely no sign of recognizing me from yesterday.

"This is a friend of my studio mate," James said hurriedly. "She stopped by to leave a note for Nina. She was just about to leave." He grabbed the note from me.

"I will give this to Nina," he said. He looked at Mimi and said quietly, "You don't have anything to worry about."

"You'd better hope I don't," Mimi said. She put on her sunglasses, even though we were inside. She wrapped the belt of her Granny-Smith-apple-colored trench coat tighter and turned up the collar. If she'd had a fedora, she would have totally looked like a cartoon spy. Well, except for the bright green coat and the fuchsia turtleneck underneath. She wasn't exactly inconspicuous.

James beckoned me to the door.

"Tell me, have we met before?" Mimi asked. Her eyes looked me over, up and down.

"Um . . ." I was about to remind her of Dorothy Powers's apartment when her cell phone rang again.

"Yes?" she said into the phone as she turned away from me. And I am not making this up, but she waved as if she were dismissing me, as if she were shooing me out the door. "No, no. He's on his way with the real one. On a bike. Trust me. It's faster this way. Traffic is terrible . . ." Mimi went toward the back of the studio to keep talking.

"I will make sure that Nina gets your note," James said. He held the door wide open for me. I can take a hint.

What the heck was Mimi Hansen doing at Studio 4? And why did she mention a bike?

"Mimi Hansen was at Nina's studio?" Mom asked. We were eating Trader Joe's burritos in Owen's dining room. The sun was heading down toward the horizon in the west, making the lower sky a warm mix of pinks and oranges that shimmered in the water of Elliott Bay. Dinner with a view. "Did Mimi see any of Nina's work?"

"Dunno," I said as I took a bite of my burrito. "It seemed like she was there to see James. They wanted me to leave."

"James? The cute dreadlocks guy? Hmm . . . he just got a space in Studio 4," Mom said. "Maybe she's mentoring him or something."

"Mimi Hansen doesn't exactly seem like the mentoring type," I said.

"Did you see his work? It's pretty fabulous. He does those bright geometries based on body organs. It sounds weird, but his paintings are amazing."

"Maybe you don't really know this guy, Mom. Because the James I met was doing street and alley scenes, not livers and kidneys. They were this intense blue. One looked like Post Alley down at the Pike Place Market. Another one reminded me of Pioneer Square. Wait. Let me show you. I mean, I can't really show you the paintings, but I did a quick sketch of the alley that looked like Post Alley."

"An interesting departure," Mom said as she studied the sketch. "Maybe James ran out of organs. And you're right; that's Post Alley. That looks like the door to Kell's Pub. Really, Hannah, this is quite good." She clicked on the TV. Even with Owen Henderson's five hundred premium channels, Mom switched to the local news on KOMO-4 to see what her college friend Mary Perez was covering. If Mary was reporting, it was usually something juicy.

"Let's go to Mary Perez for more of the story," the news anchor said.

"Oh, good. Perfect timing," Mom said.

"I'm outside the Von Hiers Gallery in the downtown neighborhood of Belltown, where a thief just stole two paintings by celebrated artist Mimi Hansen," Mary said.

"That's right around the corner!" I said excitedly.

"Shhh! I want to hear this," Mom said.

The camera had started with a close-up of Mary Perez. Now the view widened to show the VON HIERS GALLERY sign and the front of the gallery.

"I spoke with gallery manager Cleveland Mathis a few minutes ago. The paintings disappeared some time shortly before six-thirty this evening. The two stolen paintings were part of Hansen's latest *Seattle Streetscape* series. There are two things that make these paintings special. First, they're rather small, just thirteen by eleven inches. Second, each painting has a distinctly different style, use of color, and overall look. In fact, the only thing that these paintings have in common, art experts tell me, is that they are by Mimi Hansen, and they do, in fact, have that distinctive 'Mimi Hansen signature' on them. The Von Hiers Gallery had six of these Hansen paintings on display. After today's theft, only four are left."

Mary Perez paused. I knew that meant someone was talking into the little earpiece in her ear, telling her something. Mary told me how hard it is to talk into the camera at the same time as someone is talking into your ear.

"A large painted canvas wrapped in Kraft paper was delivered to the Von Hiers Gallery just before it was discovered that two Hansen paintings were missing. Since the gallery was not expecting a delivery, the package has been turned over to Seattle police for processing," Mary said, pausing briefly again as if listening to someone update her.

"Do you think the mystery package delivered to the gallery might be like the one Dorothy got?" I asked. Mom shushed me so she could keep watching the news.

Mary resumed talking. "Two days ago, a Hansen was stolen from the Mafune Gallery. And yesterday a privately owned Hansen painting never made it to the delivery destination at Belltown Towers downtown." Mary paused again, then said, "I'm told that Mimi Hansen herself just arrived at the gallery."

The camera shot widened a bit again, and there was Mimi Hansen. It had been only an hour since I'd seen her at Nina's studio, but she was wearing a completely different getup. She had a monotone thing going on now with a sleeveless gold turtleneck and lots of thick gold chains. Her face and hair kept the golden thing going to the top of her head, making all of her shimmer for the camera.

"Man, she's everywhere these days," I murmured.

"Ms. Hansen, do you have any insight into why someone would be targeting your work at three separate crime scenes this week?" Mary asked.

"It's evident to me that people in Seattle are just now beginning to realize the brilliance of my work," Mimi said, looking directly into the camera instead of at Mary. She grabbed the KOMO microphone out of Mary's hands. "I've been heralded internationally for the depth and variety of my artistic work and my interpretation of the world around us. No one can imitate my style because no one ever knows what Mimi Hansen will have next month, next week, or even tomorrow. My work in progress is always kept very secretive. I am constantly working, creating my vision. I am, as some say, inimitable. No one can reproduce my extensive body of work. The only option for an artful thief would be . . . to steal it." Mimi stopped dramatically. She gazed into the camera and slowly shook her head. "It's a shame, really. My work inspires so many people, but I didn't expect it to inspire criminals."

"Barf. Could her ego be any bigger?" I asked Owen's flat-screen TV.

Mary snatched the microphone out of Mimi's hands. "That was local artist Mimi Hansen. Two paintings by this *prolific* artist were stolen just a half hour ago from the Von Hiers Gallery downtown."

Mom laughed when Mary said "prolific." Just because someone—like a writer or an artist—produces a lot, it doesn't mean that the person is necessarily good. But somehow people seemed to think it was some kind of compliment. I was pretty sure that Mary hadn't meant it favorably.

On the TV screen we could see a wider view. Mimi was storming off, shooing away people who tried to talk to her. The camera kept backing up, showing more of the street and the people gathered around the art gallery. Mary did her regular TV-reporter sign-off: "We'll have an update for you on the eleven-o'clock news. Live from downtown Seattle, this is Mary Perez for KOMO TV. Back to you, Kathy...."

And that's when I saw them: Not one but two Swifty's bicycle messengers were in the background.

CHAPTER 13

"YOU'RE CRAZY," Lily said into the phone.

"That's irrelevant to the case," I said. "We've got to see why bike messengers are swarming all over the Seattle art scene."

"Swarming? Listen, Sherlock West, they're pedaling. That's what bike messengers do. As the offspring of a messenger, I know these things," Lily said.

I'd completely forgotten that Lily's dad, Dan, had worked his way through graduate school as a bike messenger. He always said it was the greatest job he ever had.

"Hey, could you ask your dad about it? You know, if any of this seems weird to him?"

"I can ask him, but Hannah, it might have been a little weird on the weekend, but today's a regular workday."

"Aren't most offices closed by now? It's after seven," I pointed out.

"Still, it could be just a—" Lily started to say.

"Don't say it's just a coincidence," I interrupted. Lily was silent. I guess that was exactly what she was going to say.

Either that or she was busy swallowing the Cheetos she hoards in her room to make up for her dad's daily organic dinner specials.

I knew Lily couldn't resist the appeal of a real-life mystery any more than she could resist a Miss Marple mystery. She was on the case, as far as I was concerned, and I could count on her. We made plans for her to spend the night at Belltown Towers on Friday.

"I need to get back to my trig homework. Mrs. Olson is killing me with this endless homework. Night after night after night. She piles it on," Lily said.

"Trig? What are you talking about?"

"I'm practicing what I'm going to say to my parents so they'll leave me alone and let me read in my room. They're back on their No TV on Weekdays thing. They're terribly eager to play a rousing game of gin rummy right now."

"Got it," I said. "Lily, do you even know what 'trig' is?"

"Not exactly. But I think I'll sound more convincing if I say I have trigonometry to do."

Jordan Walsh (or "Enj," as I'd decided to call her) wasn't in class the next day. Not that I'm an attendance taker or anything. It's just that it would be hard not to notice whether the new girl was there or not. It would also be hard not to notice that Zac Mason, Ryan Steinberg, and a few other guys were obviously disappointed by Jordan's absence. Geesh. You'd think that 51 percent of Chavez

Middle School—the 51 percent that was female—was invisible or something, the way the guys were talking about Jordan. Already they were referring to her as J-Dub. Lily and I had been crafty to go for Enj as her code name.

I rode the school bus home with Lily, but she had to get to a clarinet lesson, so there wasn't time to hang out with her. I headed to her house anyway. It's part of my cover. You see, if it seems like I'm just hanging out with my best friend, maybe no one will notice that Mom and I don't live in that neighborhood anymore. You wouldn't think anyone would care, but there's one pesky kid on the block who could blow it for us.

"Hi, Hannah," Dira called out to me.

And that was the kid.

"Hey, Dira," I called. Dira's mom was on the Seattle School Board. She was the one who sponsored the rule that kids needed permanent addresses to attend specific schools. She said that it was so the "poor homeless youth" wouldn't get lost in the shuffle, but the truth was that she didn't want homeless kids in class with any of her three precious children. Dira walked like her mom, talked like her mom. She wore khaki pants, a white polo shirt, and a blue jacket with a gold emblem on the chest pocket almost every day. I think it was Dira's version of an uppity private-school uniform, even though she was in the fourth grade at Olympic View Elementary, the public school up the street. She looked like a junior real-estate agent and miniversion of her mom. It was creepy.

We were two houses away from Lily's. I looked at my watch. "Oh, man. If I run now, I can catch the next bus downtown to meet my mom and hang out at the bookstore," I said to Lily.

"Okay. Call me when you get back up here to your house," Lily said. She was using her acting abilities to project her voice so it reached Dira's precious ears. "Maybe I can come over to your house after dinner," she added.

"Great. Gotta go. See you, Dira." I sprinted back to Eightieth Street just as the Metro bus pulled up. Once again, perfect timing. I jumped on and swiped my Metro pass through the ticket machine.

It wasn't until I sat down that I realized I was on the wrong bus.

It's not a total disaster to be on the wrong bus. Like I said, I have schedules and routes memorized for sixteen different buses around Seattle. But it's kind of a hassle to have to get off and transfer to another bus. Sometimes it even takes two transfers to get back on the right track.

Turns out I'd jumped onto the 67 instead of the 66. The last stop for the 67 is in the University district, a cool, funky neighborhood by the University of Washington, less than five miles north of downtown.

I got off on "The Ave," the main street running north-south in the U-district, and headed toward my next bus stop.

A cyclist whizzed past me on the sidewalk, almost knocking me out. I saw a flash of the distinctive black-and-purple jersey from Swifty's Bicycle Messengers.

The number 48 bus pulled up, but I resisted the urge to get on it, since it would be the wrong bus yet again. It pulled out, and the view across the street opened up just as two women were putting a sign in the window of the Martin Lee Gallery. I read FEATURING NEW WORK BY MIMI HA . . . The end of the sign had flopped over, so I couldn't see the end of the name. But it doesn't take a spry young detective to figure out what it said.

The number 72 pulled up, rescuing me from the urge to check out the newest Mimi Hansen exhibit.

CHAPTER 14

I WAS IN that weird zoning thing that happens when you're on a bus. You know what I mean? I was staring out the window, but I wasn't really seeing anything. I was thinking about Mimi Hansen's paintings, but I wasn't really thinking.

The bus stopped in front of a small art gallery on Eastlake Avenue. The name painted on the window read HENNINGS BOVENG GALLERY. I looked through the glass, and my eyes started to glaze over as all the paintings blurred together. Then one caught my attention.

I snapped out of my trance. I pulled the cord to tell the bus driver I wanted off at the next stop.

I said a hurried thanks to the driver, jumped down two steps, and raced two blocks back to the gallery, where I'd seen a glimpse of a most interesting painting. In fact, you might say that the painting had an interesting "play of light." Just like one that James had been working on at Studio 4.

"May I help you with something?" A man in a black

turtleneck and black pants practically jumped on me as I entered the doorway of the gallery. All of Seattle was going crazy with spring fever, and this guy was wearing black from head to toe. Maybe it was a required uniform if you worked in an art gallery.

"I just wanted to look more closely at that blue painting over there," I said. "I think a friend of mine did it."

Mr. Snotty Art Guy looked at me in disbelief.

"Well, James isn't really a good friend of mine or anything. He's a friend of a friend," I said.

"James?" Mr. Snotty Art Guy's voice went up about half an octave, and he swallowed hard.

"James shares a studio space with my friend Nina," I said rather importantly. "I was there yesterday."

Mr. Snotty Art Guy walked back to the desk and started moving papers around. "I don't know this James you mention, but you are welcome to look more closely at the painting as long as you don't touch it," he said, his voice a bit too loud for the small gallery. "Although I doubt you are in a buying mood this afternoon, are you?" he added with a bit of a sneer.

I stood up straight and flipped my hair back over my shoulder. Who was this guy to question my buying ability? Had this guy missed the memo telling him that teens hold important buying power and are the hot, in-demand consumers in the United States? Besides, what if I were as rich as Jordan Walsh, and I could actually buy a painting?

I wanted to tell this guy a thing or two, but the blues in the painting seemed to be calling me to it, inviting me to spend some time looking at it, just like when I'd first seen it downtown at Nina's studio. I couldn't stop looking at it. I stood in front of the painting, twirling a chunk of my hair, a habit I can't seem to shake. It means I'm thinking, but people always misinterpret it as a sign of nervousness. This time I was totally lost in thought. Lost in the painting.

"It's gorgeous! It looks even better out of the studio," I finally said. "You know," I added in a haughty whisper, "I was in the studio when this was created. Aren't there two others in the series?"

"Yes, there are," said Mr. Snotty Art Guy, an eyebrow arching up as he looked me up and down. I could tell I had his attention.

"Do you have the other two? I'd like to see them." Hey, I had every right to look at art, didn't I?

"Yes, miss, right this way," he said with mock humility. "Please feast your eyes on the *Seattle Streetscapes* series."

He showed me the other two paintings.

"Oh yes! Magnificent! Truly magnificent," I said, trying to act like I was some rich art-collector person. "Hmm . . . that's rather odd, isn't it?"

"What now?" Mr. Snotty Art Guy wasn't playing along with me. He sounded bored.

"There's no signature on these paintings," I replied.

"Surely you know all about that, since you seem to think

you're a close personal friend of the artist," he said with a sneer.

"I told you, he's a friend of a friend. James told me he wasn't ready to sign them," I said, resorting to my ordinary Hannah West voice.

"Who's James? Not that I really care," he said.

"Who's James?" I echoed back. Was this guy a nimrod or what? "James . . ." I realized I didn't know his last name. "You know. *James.* The artist."

"James might be an artist, but I assure you that these three paintings are Mimi Hansen originals."

"What?" I gasped.

"Surely an art aficionado like you can recognize a Hansen when you have the rare opportunity to see one," he said.

"Yesterday I was in Nina and James's studio and these paintings were there," I said.

"Perhaps this person you call James was holding the paintings for Mimi Hansen," he said.

"It didn't seem like it. He'd just finished them," I said.

"Perhaps this James was working on some imitation of the brilliant Mimi Hansen's work. Perhaps someone of your age cannot tell a fake when she sees it."

Mr. Snotty Art Guy was getting snottier by the minute. I cleared my throat.

"Could you please tell me why Mimi Hansen didn't sign these paintings?" I asked.

"She will sign these paintings after they are sold at the Honcho auction this weekend," he replied.

"Just like Dorothy Powers's painting?" I asked.

"And I suppose you know Dorothy Powers, too?" he asked.

I don't think he really wanted an answer. I thanked him for his time and kindness to a young girl interested in art. (I can be snotty, too, Mr. Snotty Art Guy.)

I walked out of the gallery and SMASH! I rammed right into someone.

"Gosh, I'm sorry," I stammered.

"Watch where you're going," snapped a female voice. A vaguely familiar female voice. Jordan Walsh's voice. Our eyes connected, and I could tell it took her another second to register who she'd collided with.

"Hey, Jordan," I said, trying my best to be genuinely friendly. "Do you live around here or something?"

"No!" she said, as if I'd insulted her. "I live on Capitol Hill now," she added, a bit more civilly.

"I'd better get going," I said. "I live downtown. In Belltown Towers," I added, trying to one up her.

I saw a flash in Jordan's eyes, but I had no idea what she was thinking.

"See you at school," she said, still avoiding eye contact.

"You must be feeling better," I said, wondering once again why I didn't stop talking and say good-bye because I had a bus to catch, which I did.

"What? No. I mean, yes. I mean, I didn't feel all that great today, but I'm getting better." I might not know Jordan Walsh very well, but I could tell that this girl was clearly uneasy. And she hadn't been sick. She was even blushing as she tried to fabricate a story. Lily always says I have an advantage because my olive-tone skin can hide embarrassment, or at least the blushing that comes with it, better than lots of other people. Jordan had a light golden tan, but the blushing still came through. A taxi driver waiting at the curb honked a horn. Jordan's blush turned scarlet.

"There's my taxi," she said.

Taxi? What sixth grader took a taxi? Oh, wait. Maybe a sixth-grade golden girl who just moved from the suburbs. I might not blush easily, but my face is like an open book. I'm sure Jordan could see what I was thinking. "It's no big deal," she said. "The taxi, that is. My dad insists on it, even though it's only about a mile to my mom's house." I nodded, like I understood completely about overprotective dads who called taxis to take their daughters twenty blocks.

Jordan got in the backseat of the yellow cab. I started walking toward the next bus stop, making sure I was looking straight ahead when the taxi passed me so we could both avoid any awkward waving moments.

Swoosh!

"What the . . ." I cried out, flattening myself against a bakery window. Three other pedestrians were nearly knocked over, too.

"Bikes belong in the street!" one guy yelled out.

Yep. You guessed it. A bike on the sidewalk. A bike powered by a Swifty's bike messenger. The same guy I'd seen on the bus and at the Stimson Building, outside Nina's studio.

I hopped on the next 72 bus heading downtown. I was supposed to meet Mom at the bookstore. I pulled out my sketch pad and turned to the drawing of the bike messenger.

I got an uneasy feeling about this guy even when I was only looking at him in 2-D.

CHAPTER 15

MOM WAVED HELLO but she was talking on her cell phone when I walked into M Coy Books. She fills in at this cool bookstore by the Pike Place Market when Michael and Michael, the owners, need extra help. I looked through a copy of *Bad Cat* near the cash register until she got off the phone.

"That was Mary Perez," Mom said. "We were going to meet for a quick walk tonight, but she's on a story. She's at the Martin Lee Gallery in the U-district—and another Mimi Hansen was just stolen!"

"I hate the way people say that!" I exclaimed, completely glossing over the fact that Mom had said that another painting had been stolen.

"What?" Mom said.

"You know, they say 'a Mimi Hansen' instead of saying 'a painting.' Like, 'a Mimi Hansen was stolen.' You just said it that way. It drives me crazy," I ranted.

"Somehow I don't think that's what's really bothering you," Mom said.

"I'm just so sick of Mimi Hansen. A week ago I'd never even heard her name. Now I hear it all the time," I said.

A customer walked up to the counter. Mom gave me the "I'll talk to you later" signal.

It took me this long to register exactly what Mom had said. A painting by Mimi Hansen had been stolen in the University district, where I'd just been. In fact, the Martin Lee Gallery was right across the street from where I'd transferred to the southbound bus.

I headed to the back where one of the Michaels was working behind the coffee bar. I sat down on a tall stool and he slid a Thomas Kemper Vanilla Crème Soda down the counter to me. I like sitting at the counter. It feels so grown up, like I'm a regular at a diner.

"Rough day, I take it?" Michael asked.

"Nah. Just an ordinary day in the life of a Seattle middle schooler on the go. I've taken four different buses to get here, and I'm still not home. Not that I even have a home. On top of that, a snotty art guy was extra-special snotty to me because I'm a kid," I whined.

Michael handed me an Uncle Seth cookie. It was one of those huge round shortbread cookies with an inch of fluffy pink frosting on top. "Mmmm . . . sugar bomb," I said, à la Homer Simpson. I gratefully bit into the cookie.

"What's the Honcho auction?" I asked Michael.

"Do you mean Humans of Northwest Cultural and Harmony Organizations?" he asked.

"Huh?" I was paying attention, but this pink frosting was divine.

"It's what Honcho stands for. It started off as a joke, making fun of the Poncho auction, where the superwealthy people buy things they don't need for outlandish prices, and it all supports the arts," he said.

"Poncho? What a dorky name for an auction," I said.

"It's an acronym, too. Patrons of Northwest Charitable something-or-other Organizations, or something like that," Michael said.

"So why do they need a Honcho auction if there was already a Poncho auction?" I asked between cookie bites.

"A bunch of MegaComp millionaires started Honcho to raise money for the fringe theater groups and undiscovered arts organizations that they thought were overlooked by Poncho. Now the Honcho auction is the biggest arts fund-raiser in the city."

"Who goes?" I asked.

"Anyone can go, as long as you guarantee that you'll spend at least two thousand dollars while you're there," he said.

"Yikes!" I exclaimed.

"Two thousand is just a drop in the bucket," Michael said. "Last year, a puppy was auctioned off for eight thousand dollars."

"For a puppy? What kind of wonder dog was it?"

"A Cavalier King Charles spaniel," Michael said.

"Those are pretty cute dogs," I said. In addition to knowing Metro bus schedules, I've also memorized *The Legacy of the Dog*, a dog-breed book that I used to look at every time I went to M Coy Books. "Still, that's a whole lot of money."

"They're predicting that some of those Mimi Hansen paintings will go for five to twenty thousand dollars apiece," said Michael. "All the recent publicity hasn't hurt, either."

Just then, another customer came and sat at the coffee bar. What are people in Seattle doing drinking coffee at six o'clock in the evening? Obviously this woman needed a double-tall nonfat latte to have the energy to get her home.

Mom came down the steps toward the coffee counter.

"I was listening to KUOW, and I heard about another Mimi Hansen painting being stolen," she said.

"The one from the U-district?" I asked.

"No. Another one. Just in the last few minutes. This last robbery was from a gallery on Eastlake."

CHAPTER 16

MOM AND I were back at Belltown Towers by 6:25 P.M. Dorothy Powers left a message inviting us up for mu shu pork. By 6:28, we were at her door. By 6:29, Mom had told her about the robberies, giving us a full minute to gather in front of the tiny TV in Dorothy's kitchen for the 6:30 news.

Mom's friend Mary was on camera in front of the art gallery where I'd just encountered Mr. Snotty Art Guy. That's right. The same gallery where I'd been less than an hour and a half ago.

"We reported earlier on the theft of a painting by Seattle artist Mimi Hansen. The painting was stolen from the Martin Lee Gallery of Local Art in the University district. Just one hour later, a second painting by artist Mimi Hansen was stolen from yet another gallery. This time the thief struck here, at the Hennings Boveng Gallery on Eastlake," Mary said. The camera backed up to show the storefront of the gallery. Then it zoomed in on Mary again.

"Seattle police are puzzled about who could sneak so swiftly into a gallery during daylight hours, boldly take a piece of artwork off the wall, and disappear without anyone noticing. Traffic was at a standstill on Eastlake Avenue when the theft occurred at the Hennings Boveng Gallery, making it nearly impossible for a getaway car to be involved. Police add that they have no leads on the case, but they have set up a special toll-free hotline for anyone who may have information on the art thefts throughout the city." An 800-number flashed on the screen.

"Hansen has taken the local art world by storm in the last few months. She is known for the wide range of her work. Many call her a prolific artist."

I glanced at Mom and saw her smirk.

"I have artist Mimi Hansen here with me now," Mary continued on TV. "Mimi, tell us a bit about your thoughts about these crimes. Why do you think someone would target your work?"

I was betting that Mary wasn't happy about having to turn over the microphone to Mimi again. Last time Mimi had grabbed the microphone out of Mary's hands and taken over the interview.

This time Mimi kept her hands off the microphone, but she clearly had a command over the camera. The camera got closer and closer as she talked.

"This is such a cruel, cruel crime," Mimi said. She took off her sunglasses and dabbed a tissue at her eyes. "Art is a precious creative statement that has the ability to reach the soul of every person. Even if they don't understand the complexity of my art, it still resonates with them on some emotional level."

Geesh. Was she being insulting or what?

"I find it hard to believe that a common criminal would have the intellectual ability to appreciate fine art like mine. I think this thief must be a cut above the rest. Obviously I am a rising star, and my art will be worth more and more every year," she continued.

"It will be worth even more now with all this publicity," Mom muttered.

"I can only hope these paintings are returned soon. Some of my work will be featured at the Honcho auction next weekend. In fact, I think it's fair to say that the Mimi Hansen paintings are the most important items at this year's auction. If you are the thief and you are watching now, I beg you to return them. Do it for the arts. Do it for Honcho," Mimi said. She put her sunglasses back on and choked back a sob.

The camera turned back to Mary. "This is Mary Perez, live on Eastlake Avenue, reporting on the most recent art theft. Back to you, Kathy."

"Oh dear," said Dorothy. She clicked off the TV. "Mimi is such a powerful artist. I hope all this publicity doesn't destroy her or weaken her artistic vision."

I remembered what Michael had said earlier.

"I think she might like all the publicity," I said. Dorothy gave me a surprised, almost dismayed look.

"She does seem to do well when all the cameras are on her, Dorothy," Mom said softly.

"Surely you don't think Mimi had anything to do with this?" Dorothy asked.

Mom and I looked at each other.

"I don't think Mimi is behind the thefts," I started to say. "I think—"

"I agree with you, Hannah," Mom said, pointedly interrupting me. "Mimi isn't stealing them. She certainly couldn't make a quick getaway with those high-heeled shoes she wears." I laughed a little. Mom realized she might have been too glib, so she quickly turned more serious. "I'm sorry. That just slipped out," she said to Dorothy. "But she does seem quite comfortable in front of a camera."

"Mimi seems to magically appear whenever there's a theft—and a TV camera," I said.

"Dear, I think that's a bit of an exaggeration," Dorothy said.

"Maybe I am exaggerating," I admitted. "Do you think Mimi used to work on TV? She seems totally into this camera thing. I don't mean that as an insult or anything," I quickly added.

Neither Mom nor Dorothy had any idea about Mimi's past. It's like six months ago an artist named Mimi Hansen didn't exist. Now she was the talk of the town as well as the toast of the town. I wonder if that was how it worked. You had to get people talking about you before you could be highly regarded for something, for anything.

We thanked Dorothy for dinner. Then Mom headed back down to Owen's apartment, and I took Ruff downstairs for a quick walk around the block. We'd just started down the street when a guy on a bike swerved wide on the sidewalk to miss us, then jumped off his bike while it was still moving, in a graceful style I now expected from bike messengers. This bike guy leaned his bike against a large blue-glazed planter near the Belltown Towers entrance. He straightened his messenger bag and a second bag that was like an artist's portfolio case. He buzzed a number on the intercom security system.

"Yes?" a voice crackled over the intercom.

"Delivery for you, Mr. Chomsky."

Bzzzzzzz.

The front door unlocked, and the same Swifty's bike messenger I'd seen at least two times before headed into the Belltown Towers. After hours. At least an hour after the last delivery time listed on Swifty's Web site. I know that because I checked. No weekend deliveries. No evening deliveries.

Except to Belltown Towers?

CHAPTER 17

I TOOK RUFF for a quick loop around the block. I went back up to thirteen and was just getting off the elevator when the door to PH-2 quickly closed. It hadn't been open far. It was as if Mr. Chomsky was checking out the action, seeing who was getting off the elevator. That gave me an idea.

I knocked softly on Mr. Chomsky's door. I stood back from the door and directly in line with the peephole so he could see me. I had a hunch he'd probably been looking through it the entire time anyway.

"Yes?" I heard his voice from the other side of the door.

"Mr. Chomsky? I'm a friend of Dorothy's? Your neighbor across the hall?" Yee gads. My voice was going up at the end of each sentence, like I was asking questions. Time to change to a more assertive tone. "My name is Hannah. I'm her dog walker. I was wondering if I could ask you something."

The door opened a crack. "Something about what? Please be more specific when making an information request," he said.

"Well, I wanted to ask you about delivery services," I said. "I'm working on a social-studies project on different service professions, and I thought I'd see if you ever used UPS, FedEx, or any other kind of services for deliveries . . . maybe even bike messengers?" I hoped I'd been smooth and subtle.

The door opened. "I don't often get visitors," he said. "I'll leave the door open, and we can talk right here." He didn't say that in a cranky way like someone might if they didn't want to invite you inside. Quite the opposite. I think he had impeccable manners, as he must have recognized that my mom would go absolutely ballistic if her daughter went into a stranger's apartment.

And what an apartment! Even from the doorway I could tell it was the mirror image of Dorothy's, but while Dorothy's was full of old-world charm and art and cozy rugs and overstuffed chairs, Mr. Chomsky's apartment was supertechy mixed with the decor of an overcrowded library. Books covered almost every inch of his walls, as well as every flat surface available, including the floor, where more books were precariously stacked into two- and three-foot piles. At least a half-dozen easels were scattered throughout the living room, some with paintings in their frames and some with unframed canvases. Even with the overabundance of books, the place seemed clean and organized. There seemed to be order to the chaos.

There was one spot on the wall where a large plasma screen replaced the books. It looked as if the bookcase had been custom-built to allow for the screen's exact dimensions. Apparently the plasma screen was also his computer monitor, because instead of seeing a television show, the screen was full of a word-processing document. He must have noticed I noticed it, because he took a device out of the pocket of his shirt and whispered into it, "Change screen." The screen switched to a crisp photograph of a tulip field.

I'd expected Mr. Chomsky to be one of two ways: a wild-haired Einstein kind of guy in a bathrobe or a stuffy-looking British guy who wears bow ties all the time, even when playing tennis, which of course he would never do because he never left his apartment. Both of my visions of Mr. Chomsky were wrong. He was dressed pretty normal, with Levi's, a bright white cotton turtleneck with the sleeves pushed up to his elbows, and shiny cowboy boots. He had short gray hair and a clean-shaven face.

"This isn't about social studies, is it?" he asked, and he smiled. It was a genuine smile that you could see was sincere because of the way his eyes seemed to be smiling, too. If I'd expected this hermit to be a deranged old man, I was wrong. Ruff seemed at ease here, too, and so far his instincts had been spot on. Still, I stayed in the doorway in case my own assessment was wrong.

"No, it isn't about social studies. Unless you want to talk about the Byzantine Empire, which is what we're studying right now," I admitted.

"Interesting subject, the Byzantine Empire," he said. "But I suspect that something else has piqued your curiosity."

I was pretty curious about why this cowboy-boot-wearing man stayed in his apartment all the time, but I had enough basic manners under my belt to know I couldn't just blurt out questions about that. "Actually, I want to know about bike messengers," I said. "Dorothy said you have messengers deliver stuff to you."

"That I do. Are you looking to supplement your dog-walking business?" he asked.

"Um, no. I'm just wondering. Did you have a messenger deliver something to you this past Sunday?"

"Sunday? No, no, no. I've tried every bike-messenger service in Seattle, and no one seems to want to work on Sundays. Not even on Saturdays. In this town, it's strictly weekdays."

"Even Swifty's bike messengers?" I asked.

"Especially Swifty's," Mr. Chomsky said. "I used them for years, but they cut back their service hours. No deliveries after six P.M. and no deliveries on weekends."

"Interesting," I said, mulling this over, stalling for time like Columbo from that 1970s detective show. "I thought I just saw a Swifty's bike messenger make a delivery here."

"Oh no, my dear. I'm sure you didn't see a messenger

coming here after-hours," Mr. Chomsky said with a wink. "Now, if you don't mind, I need to get back to my research. If you decide you want to discuss the Byzantine Empire, please come back. It's not my primary research focus these days, but I did devote a few years during the 1950s to it," he said. His manner, although still friendly, turned abrupt.

"Research?" I must have looked dumbfounded.

"Yes. I need to get back to my research," he said again.

"Well, thank you," I said, bending down to scoop up Ruff. It was an artful ploy to give me a chance to stall and look one last time inside his apartment.

"Aaahhhh . . ." I started to gasp. "I mean, aaaah-choooo . . ." I faked a sneeze.

I'd just seen two large, flat packages wrapped in plain brown paper leaning against Mr. Chomsky's worktable, right alongside a country landscape with the name Mimi Hansen scrawled in the lower right corner.

CHAPTER 18

AS SOON AS I got home, I called Lily to discuss this latest development in the case. It was pretty clear that Mr. Chomsky was hiding something with his off-hours messenger deliveries. And what was with those wrapped-up paintings? Did he have something to do with the thefts?

"And why do I keep seeing the same bike messenger all the time?" I asked Lily.

"Twice? You've seen this guy twice, and you call that *all the time*?" she asked.

"I think it's been three times. And I think it's significant. Three is always significant. Like that blue painting I saw in Nina's studio. The one that I thought James painted, but the rest of the world says Mimi Hansen painted. I've seen that same painting three times now. Three times! That's significant."

"I'd say *weird* would be a better word choice than *significant*," Lily said.

"It's even weirder that it's a Mimi Hansen painting," I said. "Something isn't quite right. It really seemed like it was part of James's work at the studio. And why do I keep seeing bike messengers?"

"Do you know how many messenger companies there are in Seattle?" Lily asked.

"No, but I think you're about to tell me."

"That's right. I am. There are eleven. And Swifty's isn't even the biggest, according to my dad."

"And all of this supports the total significance of me seeing Swifty's bike messengers repeatedly," I said.

"Maybe you notice them more because they wear purple. You've had this thing for purple ever since we were in second grade."

She had me there.

"We need to get back on track with our case," I said.

"It's not like you've been hired to solve this or something," Lily said, as if that somehow needed clarifying.

"That's what makes us the perfect sleuths. No one notices teen girls."

"We're sleuths? We're teens?"

"Yes, we're sleuths. And we're almost teens."

"Cool. Let's look at this James guy. Maybe Mimi is working on some top-secret project with him at that studio," Lily said.

"Nina can't keep a secret. I think if Mimi Hansen were working in her studio, she'd spill the beans. She definitely would have told Mom. And Mom would have said something to me," I said.

"Parents can keep secrets, you know," Lily said.

"Some parents can keep secrets. But Maggie West can't," I countered.

"Okay. Let's say that Mimi wasn't using that studio. Maybe James saw Mimi's work and was copying it," Lily said.

"But Mimi stopped by the studio yesterday," I said. "If James is imitating her work, he's totally busted."

"That brings us back to the theory that she uses the Studio 4 space to paint."

Lily's theory that Mimi painted in the same space as Nina wasn't exactly taking hold of my imagination. But *Frankenstein* was. I stayed up late reading for my English quiz the next day. I have to admit that I thought Frankenstein was a zombie guy with bolts in his neck. And even though I'd heard people refer to it as "Frankenstein's monster," in the original story the monster is nameless.

Sort of like Mimi Hansen paintings. They might have titles, but they're nameless. Or signatureless.

CHAPTER 19

THE 6:30 DISCO alarm came way too early Friday morning. I woke up expecting to be a character in some gothic novel. But then I looked out Owen Henderson's window at the Bainbridge Island ferryboat crossing Elliott Bay, and I snapped back to the twenty-first-century reality.

I didn't give Mimi Hansen a second thought. Heck, I hadn't even thought about Jordan Walsh. But then I got to Chavez Middle School. That's when I saw Mimi Hansen's little white convertible zip past me and park in the bus zone. And get this: A Channel 4 News camera was pointed right at her when she pulled up.

The camera person came closer to the car. Mimi hopped out and smoothed her skirt. Jordan got out on her side, tossing her backpack over her shoulder and putting on sunglasses.

The vice principal gets a little testy whenever someone parks in the bus-loading zone. But I hardly think it's newsworthy. Something was definitely up.

"You're never going to guess who's here," I said to Lily. We met at our regular spot, the spindly maple tree at the Fifth Avenue side of Chavez Middle.

"Let me guess. Channel 4 News?" Lily said.

"Well, yeah, them, too. But that isn't who I'm talking about. Mimi's here."

Lily didn't seem to connect right away.

"Mimi Hansen is at school. And so is a news crew."

"What's up with that?" Lily asked.

"I think we're about to find out," I said. Grace Malone, the mouth of the middle school, headed straight for us.

"What's up, Grace?" I asked.

"You'll never guess why Channel 4 is here!" Grace oozed with excitement.

"Are they here to give you the Perkiest Student Award?" I asked. When Grace giggled, I kind of hated myself for being sarcastic to her.

"You know about all those paintings by that famous artist that have been stolen?" Grace whispered.

We nodded encouragingly.

"Well, it turns out that Jordan Walsh is her daughter! Channel 4 is doing one of those human-interest thingies, you know, where they follow people around to show how famous people are really ordinary and all that. So they're getting some shots of Mimi and Jordan at school," said Grace. "I bet I can guess the angle they'll take. It will be all about how Jordan is a budding genius artist, too. This is soooo exciting!"

Lily and I rolled our eyes at each other. I could tell that Grace was thinking over what kind of things she could say on camera, just in case the Channel 4 News crew decided to interview one of Jordan's classmates.

I'm not a TV expert or anything, but I'm pretty sure that following a middle-school student's mother around Chavez Middle wasn't going to be a ratings hit. The crew was probably just getting a few shots of Mimi letting her daughter off at school, and that was it.

Boy, was I wrong.

"Oh, brother," I murmured. A camera was aimed right at each of us as we entered the art studio.

Jack Finster made a face into the camera. Demi Demick gave a peace sign. And I, Hannah West, looked at my shoes and walked into the classroom as quickly as possible. I'm sure we all made fascinating TV.

A woman wearing a red suit jacket and tons of makeup was talking to Ms. Murdoch at the front of the room. Ms. Murdoch was smiling and nodding, but she looked a little tense. Maybe she was worried that she'd end up on TV or something.

"Class, we have a reporter here from Channel 4 News today," Ms. Murdoch said. That explained why the red-jacket woman was wearing so much makeup. "They're doing a story on Jordan's mother, Mimi Hansen, and how she volunteers to help at Chavez Middle School's arts programs."

Huh? Mimi Hansen volunteered at school? This was Jordan's first week at this school. Besides, Mimi didn't seem like a PTA mom or the kind of mom who helped out in the classroom. Especially not in middle school, when no self-respecting student would allow a parent inside the school. But there she was, wearing a big blue work shirt with the sleeves all rolled up, like she was ready to finger-paint with us or something.

Ms. Murdoch told us we'd be sketching a still life that Mimi had arranged for us. She aimed some lights at the worktable, lighting up a Buddha, a pyramid, and a tall vase with spiky branches coming out.

"Try walking around the room and looking at this from all angles," Mimi called to us, but she was really talking into the camera.

The camerawoman followed Jordan as she slowly circled the room. Each time she stopped, the camera-woman zoomed over to the still life, as if trying to see what Jordan might be seeing.

"You know, I just don't get into the classroom as much as I'd like," Mimi Hansen said to the reporter.

"How often do you help in your daughter's school?" the reporter asked.

"Try 'never,'" I heard someone say. Could it be? Yes! Those words of truth came from Jordan Walsh herself. I'd assumed that Jordan was totally digging this TV thing. But she actually looked mortified.

"What was that?" the reporter asked, looking around the room.

"I said, 'not often enough,'" Mimi said through a clenched-teeth smile.

"Jordan, as you know, your mom won't allow us into her private studio at your home. Can you tell us what it's like to work on art projects side by side at your home studio?" the reporter asked with a blindingly white smile.

"Actually, Mom doesn't—" Jordan began.

Mimi rushed over to Jordan's side. "We really like to keep our home life private, don't we, honey?" Mimi said. I think she meant Jordan when she said "honey," but she was talking directly to the reporter.

I was paying way too much attention to all this. I tried concentrating on Buddha.

Suddenly the room got darker. I looked up and realized that the TV lights had turned off. Mimi flounced out of the room.

"'Bye, Mom," I heard Jordan call.

Mimi turned and gave a dramatic wave. "Good-bye, darling," she said with a smile. But the smile and the wave were aimed at the TV camera, not at her daughter.

I had an icky feeling in my stomach. I wanted to look at Jordan, but I didn't want to. I looked anyway.

She was bent over her sketch pad. But I could tell she was crying.

I couldn't believe it. I actually felt sorry for Jordan Walsh.

CHAPTER 20

JORDAN WASN'T IN social studies or language arts. Grace Malone told Mr. Ogata it was because she was busy being interviewed for a prime-time TV special.

"Thank you for the update, Grace," Mr. Ogata said. "I'll make a note of that right next to the column where I'm marking her absent."

I was thinking about Jordan so much that when I did finally see her at lunch, I had to say something.

"Hey," I said. I was trying to put a lot of compassion and kindness into that one-word greeting.

"Is it okay if I sit here?" Jordan asked. She was sitting on the stoop where Lily and I usually hang out in the morning and where I like to sit and sketch during lunch. "I mean, I know this is your spot and everything. I just don't feel like being down there." She motioned toward the bed of social activity in the main lunchroom.

"It's cool," I said. "Want a taquito?"

"No, but thanks," Jordan said. "What do you draw when you're sitting here?"

"Just regular stuff," I said. I didn't mention the recent sketch of her as Medusa. "You know, I just have to keep drawing." I glanced at her. "Do you feel like that? Like you have to draw?"

"Um, I don't think I'm actually very artistic," Jordan said.

"You must be, or you wouldn't be in Ms. Murdoch's art class," I said. Geesh. I hadn't known I could be so polite and supportive.

"Ms. Murdoch asked to have me in her class. I have no idea why."

"Maybe she thinks you're genetically programmed to be an artist," I said. "You know, because of your mom and all."

"Pleeeeeze," Jordan said. "Mom wasn't born an artist. She just became one. In fact, when she broke up with my stepdad, she thought all artists were airhead idiots. But maybe that's because my stepdad had an affair with an artist."

"Really?" I said, in what I hoped was an encouraging tone to keep her going. I was part nosy and part sincere.

"Yeah. Mom was all wrapped up in being a hotshot public-relations person. She worked all the time. All she talked about was Wentworth Enterprises. My stepdad was a Wentworth. But he was never at work. He wasn't at home, either. He was having an affair with a twenty-two-year-old art student who won a design competition for the new Wentworth logo. My stepdad got a new logo and a new wife. Mom got a divorce and a washed-up career." Jordan delivered this family history with a monotone voice.

"That's brutal," I said. "Maybe your mom used art to work through her problems, or something."

"If she did, I sure never saw her do it. She was telling that Channel 4 reporter about how private she is about her studio at home. It's so private that I've never even seen it," she said.

"You mean, it's locked and you can't go in?"

"I mean that there isn't even a studio at our house," Jordan said. "Not at our old house in Bellevue and not in our new house here in Seattle."

I had a clear picture of Jordan from her downcast eyes and the way she was talking. She might be a rich kid from the suburbs, but she was also a shy kid at a new school.

"I have to go now," Jordan said, looking uncomfortable.

"Sure. Later," I said.

I made it back to the apartment at Belltown Towers after school without witnessing any art crimes. I'd call that a successful day. Mom was sitting at the dining-room table with her laptop computer. She had her back to the window so that she wouldn't be distracted by the view of the water and the ferryboats. I knew that meant she was on a deadline.

"What are you working on?" I asked. I grabbed a Granny Smith apple from the refrigerator.

"Calendar listings for *Art Voice*," she said, without looking up. Once a month she writes a column that gives previews of all the visual-arts shows going on up and down the West Coast. Her column is called "The West View." (Clever title, isn't it? I thought of it.) Mom's column has quite a following.

"This is just unbelievable," she grumbled.

"What's unbelievable?" I asked.

"Seven different galleries have planned Mimi Hansen shows this summer. They all claim that they'll have 'new, never-before-viewed' pieces by her," Mom said, shaking her head in bewilderment. "It just doesn't seem possible that one person could create so much."

"Or be so *prolific*?" I asked.

"She's prolific, all right," Mom said. "The mind-boggling part is, so far, what I've seen, her stuff is actually good. It's so varied. It's like she's twenty different artists all at once."

"Interesting," I said. "Maybe she has multiple personalities and each one paints differently." Interesting, indeed.

"That could be one explanation, if this were a made-for-TV movie or something," Mom said. "The only thing I can think of is that maybe she was secretly working for years and years, and she just didn't show anyone her work."

"I don't think so," I said. "My multiple-personality theory would seem more likely after what I learned today."

I told Mom about what Jordan told me at lunch.

"Wow. That's a heavy load for a kid," Mom said. She got up to get a cup of tea. I sat down at her laptop and Googled *Mimi Hansen, Wentworth Enterprises,* and *Walsh.*

"Even if she doesn't have multiple personalities, it looks like she's had multiple names," I said. "Did you ever hear of Mimi Wentworth? She used to be married to some guy named Wentworth. There's a whole bunch of articles here about Mimi Walsh Wentworth and the Mills Brothers campaign."

"I remember reading about Mimi Wentworth! She was a PR person for Mills Brothers, a business that landed a bunch of high-power executives in jail," Mom said. "A lot of MegaComp millionaires invested their money in Mills Brothers, which was supposed to be a company to rival both Starbucks and Amazon. I don't remember the details, just that it was a big fat fraud. Mimi Wentworth got people to invest money in nothing."

"But nothing happened to Mimi Wentworth?" I asked.

"She just sort of dropped out of sight," Mom said.

"Until now," I said. I showed Mom the computer screen. I'd placed a photo of Mimi Wentworth, the marketing genius, next to Mimi Hansen, the artist. I hadn't been able to find a photo of Mimi Hansen without her sunglasses, though.

They looked like two completely different people. Mimi Wentworth had big hair. Really big hair. She had big lips, too. But mostly she had lots and lots of makeup on.

"Now watch this," I said.

I went into Photoshop and took the photo of Mimi Wentworth. I changed her long auburn curly hair to a chin-length straight blond style. I made her lips smaller and a lighter color. I toned down her makeup.

"Getting closer . . ." Mom said.

Then I put dark sunglasses on her to cover her blue eyes.

"Bingo!" Mom said.

CHAPTER 21

NOW I KNEW that Mimi Hansen used to be Mimi Wentworth.

So what, right? I knew it meant something. I just wasn't sure what.

The big Mimi question remained: How in the world did Mimi Hansen create so many paintings so quickly?

I headed up the fire stairs to the penthouse floor to pick up Ruff. I opened the door to the thirteenth floor just as someone with a Swifty's-bike-messenger jersey disappeared behind the elevator's closing doors.

"Dorothy!" I ran to the door of Dorothy Powers's apartment and rang the doorbell.

"Come in if you're Hannah," she called.

"I don't think that's the safest way to answer the door," I said as I walked into her apartment. "Is everything okay in here? Did you just get something delivered?"

"I'm fine, dear. But nothing was delivered," Dorothy called from the couch. She had her right leg propped up over the side of the couch. I knew she was having knee trouble and that she tried to elevate her leg as much as possible.

"I just saw a bike messenger in the hall get on the elevator."

"There must have been a delivery to Marvin Chomsky across the hall. He has messengers deliver everything to him, even toilet paper," Dorothy said. "But mostly his deliveries are for his research and his groceries."

"Just what exactly does Mr. Chomsky research?" I asked.

"He's an art historian. Quite famous in his field, I believe," Dorothy said. "Apparently he's in great demand all over the world."

"But he never leaves his apartment?" I asked.

"Not that I know of," Dorothy said. "He's mentioned museums from Oslo and Amsterdam that send him paintings to research since he won't travel to them."

"He doesn't even come across the hall?" I asked.

"He's turned down all my offers to come over for coffee."

"Maybe he's holding out for a dessert invitation," I said.

"Maybe he is." Dorothy chuckled.

"Ready for your walk, boy?" I asked the little terrier. Ruff ran to the kitchen and got his leash. I'd trained him to do that in just two sessions. "Such a good boy," I said, rewarding him with a dried-liver treat.

"I'll see you later, Dorothy," I called as Ruff tugged at his leash. "Keep your knee propped up. I'll get Ruff tuckered out for you."

Ruff loves to walk, and he's pretty fast for a little guy. But the vet had said he was a few pounds overweight. I was under strict orders not to let people feed him on our walks. This turned out to be the toughest part of the job. Ruff knows almost everyone in the Belltown neighborhood. And almost everyone wants to give him a treat.

We headed south on First Avenue. There are lots of restaurants on First Avenue with outside eating areas, but it was too early for the after-work crowd. Restaurant workers were just setting up the outside tables. It was safe territory for Ruff at 4:30, but in about thirty minutes I'd have to pick a different route if I didn't want him to go crazy wanting bits of bread or food from people's plates.

We stopped at a little park on Second and Bell. It was one of Ruff's favorite sniffing areas. There were always people and dogs at the park. Ruff sniffed his hello to seven dogs. We were just leaving the park when a cyclist on the sidewalk cruised past us, almost mowing down Ruff.

"Use the street!" I screamed. Geesh. Another cyclist cut around a corner sharply. Ruff jumped back and yelped.

"Come on! You guys aren't supposed to be on the sidewalk!" I yelled.

I started yelling before I really looked at who was pedaling. I saw the familiar purple and black. A Swifty's bicycle messenger. The rider turned around and glared at me, and then he zipped around the corner. The same guy I'd seen three times before. It figures.

"If a crime happens right here, right now, it's definitely not a coincidence," I muttered to Ruff. I looked around and listened, as if waiting for a frenzy of activity and the wail of sirens. Nothing.

Ruff and I were right by Wired Café. I looked through the window, but there was a glare from the sun, and I couldn't really see who was inside. I could tell there were some people in line for coffee. I peeked through the doorway and saw Nina working behind the espresso counter. She looked up and waved me in. I pointed down to Ruff. I couldn't go inside with a dog. Nina held up three fingers. That meant to hang on for three minutes and she'd come outside. I signaled back "okay" with three fingers up.

Wired keeps a bowl of dog water outside, and Ruff eagerly lapped some up.

"We'll need to have everything ready for Mimi to review later tonight at The Factory." A voice traveled outside through the open door. The voice sounded vaguely familiar, but I couldn't place it.

"She wasn't at all happy when she stopped by the studio earlier this week," said a man with a Jamaican accent.

"I just don't know how much longer we can keep working at this pace," the first voice said.

Two people came outside, each clutching a Wired Café cup. Ms. Murdoch, my art teacher, stopped when she saw me.

"Hannah! What fun to see you outside of school!" she

said. "I'd like you to meet my friend James."

"I believe we met at the studio," James said. "You are a friend of Nina's, right?"

I wanted to blurt out "Yes, I saw you at your studio when you were painting the *Seattle Streetscapes*, which looked suspiciously like a trio of paintings by Mimi Hansen." But I didn't get a chance because Ms. Murdoch put her arm around someone who had just arrived at Wired. Someone in a purple-and-black Swifty's jersey. "And this is my brother, Conner," Ms. Murdoch said.

Her brother held out his hand. "Conner Murdoch. I think we've run into each other around town," he said. "Or at least I almost ran into you a couple of times."

Conner Murdoch was the same cyclist who'd almost just plowed over Ruff. The same one I'd seen outside the Hennings Boveng Gallery. The same one I'd seen in the background of the news and in front of my building the other night. The same one I'd drawn in my sketch pad on Monday.

Was he the same one I'd seen outside Belltown Towers the day we'd moved in?

CHAPTER 22

NINA CAME OUT with a Mexican hot chocolate for me. It doesn't matter how hot or how cold it is, I am a sucker for this concoction of semisweet chocolate, cinnamon, vanilla bean, and cream. It's nothing like the instant hot cocoa with dehydrated minimarshmallows we have at home. Nina says she makes it special for me because she's part Mexican, but it's actually a regular drink on the Wired menu. She brought a big dog-cookie dog treat for Ruff. I vowed I'd walk him another ten minutes to make up for veering from his diet.

"Are you guys leaving now?" Nina asked Ms. Murdoch and James. "I'll catch up with you at The Factory tonight. I'll be there for a while before I have to come back here to close Wired."

The three of them left.

"You know my art teacher?" I asked.

"It's a small town if you're an artist," Nina said. "It seems like we all know each other."

"Is her brother an artist?"

"No, but he's into it," Nina said. "I guess he knows Mimi Hansen and lots of gallery folks. I don't really know much about him. He's cute, isn't he?"

"I keep seeing him around. Usually right around the same time that the paintings disappear," I said. "Look, I even sketched him a couple of times."

"Hmm . . . pretty good, Hannah. Maybe you agree with me and you think Conner Murdoch is a hottie." Nina smiled and winked at me.

"Ewwww! He's old, Nina!"

"Not too old for me. Besides, I'm sure it's just a coincidence that you keep seeing him. Swifty's headquarters is just over on Wall Street, so it makes sense you'd see him around here."

"Maybe," I reluctantly agreed. It was time to get back home if I wanted to have dinner with Mom before she left for work at Wired.

When I got into the lobby of Belltown Towers, a large, flat parcel wrapped in brown paper caught my attention. What can I say? I'm like a magnet for these packages these days. And this one was just leaning next to the mailboxes. It was addressed to Mr. Chomsky, with no return address. Time for me to be a Good Samaritan.

I wrestled the three-foot-by-three-foot package onto the elevator and pushed the "PH" button. I lugged the parcel down the hallway and breathlessly knocked on PH-2.

"Hannah!" Mr. Chomsky said warmly. "Did you decide to come back to discuss Byzantine history?"

"Not yet. I have a package for you," I said. "Don't they usually bring packages up to you?"

"It's different with every service." He sighed.

I decided not to beat around the bush anymore. "So, Mr. Chomsky, what's being delivered to you these days?"

"Usually musty old documents and paintings," he said. "Museums hire me to research the history and authenticity of paintings from all around the world. Lately I've been researching the origins of some local contemporary paintings. It's a case you might be a bit familiar with."

All of my suspicions about Mr. Chomsky being the art thief dissipated. He seemed as authentic as they come. I looked past him into the living room filled with paintings and books. My eyes stopped on the same blue painting I'd seen in his apartment the other night.

"Is that a Mimi Hansen?" I asked. "I mean, is that a painting by Mimi Hansen?" I asked more correctly.

"Ah, a good question, Miss West, no matter how you choose to frame it," Mr. Chomsky laughed at his pun. "Also, an excellent question no matter how you phrase it. As you may have noticed, there is no signature on this painting. But perhaps the signature would not tell us the truth anyway. It seems that at this point in time, this painting's origins are a bit of a mystery."

As you can tell by now, I love a mystery.

＊

"Surprise!" Lily called when I walked into our apartment.

"Hey, what are you doing here? How'd you get here?" I asked.

"Dad was meeting a friend at the Belltown Pub, so he gave me a ride down here early for our big overnight extravaganza," she said.

"Cool! Mom has to work tonight. We can hang out in Belltown and stay out late!" I said.

"Wait a minute there," Mom said. Her laptop was put away, and she was wearing her Wired uniform. They don't really have uniforms, but Mom has a definite look when she's working at Wired. Tonight it was a pink tie-dyed tank top with one of those long slinky sarong-style skirts that tie. She had on big black Dr. Martens boots, which she insisted on wearing if she was on her feet for a long shift. Her massive blond curly hair was in a ponytail on the top of her head. She has to keep her hair up or she'll start playing with it, twirling it just like I do (she says she's not sure if I got it from her or she got it from me). I watched as she put in her earrings, which takes a while since she has four piercings on one ear and seven on the other.

"I know you're kidding about being out late, but we need to go over some ground rules, girls," she said. "Belltown is crazy on Friday nights. You can come down to Wired if you want to hang out for a while. You'll need to call me to tell me when you're leaving Belltown Towers so I'll know when you'll be at Wired. Then you'll need to get back here before it gets dark. You can stay up as late as you can stand it, as long as you're in pajamas and have your teeth brushed and flossed by ten o'clock."

Nothing like a mother to put you in your place. Even a mother with eleven ear piercings.

Lily's dad had given her thirty dollars to order Chinese food. We were sitting on Owen's balcony looking at the water.

"I could get used to you guys living here," Lily said. "It's so exciting to be downtown. I can pretend we're in New York or something."

"Yes, dahling, 'tis magnificent here," I drawled. I put on sunglasses and handed a pair of Mom's to Lily. The view from Belltown Towers was truly incredible, but it faced west, and the sun was right in our eyes.

"What kind of action do you see on the street down there?" Lily asked.

"I don't really look down that much," I admitted. "It makes me kind of dizzy. I almost threw up the first day we were here."

Lily stood on the edge of the balcony and peered over. My stomach fluttered just watching her be that close. She was looking straight down at the sidewalk. "Well, you're not missing much down there," she said. "Wait! Isn't that Nina?"

I carefully looked down, my sweaty palms clutching the balcony railing. She's kind of easy to pick out in a crowd, especially when she's wearing her hair loose like it was tonight. Her thick, wavy hair fell past her shoulders. Its near-jet-blackness was a stark contrast to the tight white T-shirt she was wearing.

"It is. I wonder what she's doing here. She knows Mom is working tonight," I said.

But Nina didn't stop at Belltown Towers. She crossed the street and went to the middle of the block. She paused in front of a black door. Then she went inside.

"Do you think she has a hot date?" Lily asked.

I reached for another potsticker. "Believe me, if we were living close to a guy Nina liked, chances are she'd move in here with us. But she hasn't been hanging around much at all. Mom says she's busy with some project."

"Maybe that's her project right down there," Lily said.

A guy was definitely waiting outside the same black door that Nina had just entered. I grabbed the minibinoculars that Owen kept on top of the bookcase.

"Uh-oh," I said.

"What? Who is it? What's he look like?" Lily grabbed the binoculars from me. "Big deal. It's just a bike messenger from Swifty's." She lowered the binoculars and turned to look at me. "Come on, Hannah. It's probably just a coincidence. This guy probably just has a delivery to make to whatever business is across the street."

"It's after seven on a Friday night," I pointed out.

Lily looked through the binoculars again. "Mr. Bike Messenger is kind of cute. Is this the same guy you've been seeing all around town? You never said anything about him being cute."

"Yes! Will you listen to me? It's the same guy. And get this: He's Ms. Murdoch's brother," I said. "His name is Conner. Nina thinks he's cute, too."

"It looks like maybe Nina does have a hot date," Lily said. She handed the binoculars back to me. Nina had answered the door across the street and was holding it open for Conner Murdoch to go inside.

"Let's go see where they're going," I said.

"Ick. If they're on a date, we can't go spy on them," Lily said.

"But what if they're not on a date? What if he's about to steal a Mimi Hansen painting and Nina's in the wrong place at the wrong time?"

"Highly unlikely."

"Yet you're entertaining the possibility," I countered.

Dog walking is excellent for undercover work. Five minutes later, Lily, Ruff, and I were out the front door of Belltown Towers.

"Oops. Forgot something," I said, and turned right back into the lobby. I dragged Ruff back in after me. Lily followed grudgingly. "What's up?" she started. I put my finger to my lips. "Shhh! Step back so that guy doesn't see us."

It was Mr. Snotty Art Guy from the Hennings Boveng Art Gallery. He was still wearing a black turtleneck, black pants, a black jacket, and even black sunglasses. "Hello. The sun is on its way down. What's with the glasses?" Lily whispered.

"What's with the whispering?" I whispered back. "It's not like he can hear us out there."

Mr. Snotty Art Guy was carrying a big flat artist's portfolio, the kind with the handles on top. He jaywalked across First Avenue.

"He must not be from Seattle," Lily said.

"I was just going to say that!" I said. No one jaywalks in Seattle. Cops on bikes give out tickets like crazy when people try to cross the street without a "Walk" signal. No one crosses in the middle of a downtown street. No one but Mr. Snotty Art Guy, that is.

"He's heading for that same door," I said. "Come on!" I motioned to Lily and Ruff. We headed back out on the sidewalk. Mr. Snotty Art Guy looked like he had just rung the bell across the street. He said something into the intercom. He was pacing in front, smoking a cigarette. The door opened and he headed in.

"Okay. You've convinced me. We have to check this out!"

I said. We crossed the street and went up to the black door. The nameplate by it was blank.

"Hannah! What are you doing here? And is that Lily Shannon?"

We turned to see Ms. Murdoch, my art teacher.

CHAPTER 23

"Ms. Murdoch!" I said.

"What are you girls doing in Belltown on a Friday night?" she asked.

"Mom and I are . . ." I almost told her about the house-sitting gig we had at Belltown Towers. But Lily grabbed Ruff from me.

"Hannah and I are visiting a friend, Owen, who lives in Belltown Towers across the street," she said.

"Right," I chimed in. "Owen asked us to walk his friend's dog. This is Ruff. Remember, you saw him at Wired this afternoon? He needs to walk a lot."

"What are you up to tonight, Ms. Murdoch?" Lily asked.

"Oh, I'm on my way to a party here," she said. She didn't look like she was going to a party. She was wearing overalls with paint splatters on them, sneakers with rips in them. Her hair was in two braids, and she had a red bandanna tied over the top of her head. "I know. I know. My students never like to think I have a life after school or that I might go to a party," Ms. Murdoch was saying, a bit too enthusiastically if you ask me.

"Well, have fun, then," I said lamely.

"Rock on," Lily added. Even lamer.

"We'll just head on our walk now," I said.

We walked a few steps away and heard Ms. Murdoch whisper something into the intercom. Someone buzzed her in.

"Excuse me, will you?" a haughty voice said. We looked up to see that we'd almost run into Mimi Hansen. Of course, she didn't recognize me. She barely even acknowledged that Lily and I were human beings. We were in her way, and that was inconvenient for her.

"Sorry," we both said meekly. We walked a few more yards down the street and then slyly looked behind us to see Mimi go through that same black door.

"We've got to get into that building," I said emphatically.

"And you've got to take me with you when you get in," said a voice behind us.

I turned to see Jordan Walsh.

"Jordan?" I asked in disbelief. "What are you doing down here?"

"I'm supposed to meet my dad at Mama's Mexican Kitchen. But he's running late, as usual. So I guess my mom's going to be stuck with me for a while," she said. "She told me she'd be here in case of an emergency, but she wouldn't tell me what was going on. I guess this is an emergency, though, since she can't expect me to hang around downtown for an hour all by myself. I'm going inside to find out what's up."

"Maybe it's just a party," Lily said.

"I don't think so," Jordan said. "She was acting a little too weird for it to be just a party. I have to find out what she's hiding." She started to look a little weepy.

"You've watched them in there before, haven't you?" I asked Jordan.

"Not here," Jordan said. "But yeah, I have watched them. I was never really sure what was going on, though."

"Watched who?" Lily asked.

"The artists?" I asked gently.

She nodded again. "The real artists."

"I thought so," I said. It all made sense to me now. Someone else was creating the valuable paintings that were being sold as "Mimi Hansens."

"Is this The Factory?" I asked Jordan, remembering the conversation I'd overheard Ms. Murdoch have at Wired Café.

Jordan nodded yet again.

Just then the door opened. All of us instinctively ducked into the doorway of Sticky Fingers Bakery.

Mr. Snotty Art Guy and Conner Murdoch were on the sidewalk. "I didn't know your sister was part of The Factory crew," Mr. Snotty Art Guy said. "I guess Mimi Hansen's got the whole family on the payroll now."

"I didn't know Shelley was working for Mimi, either,"

Conner said. "It seems like the whole city is."

"I gotta go to Ralph's," Mr. Snotty Art Guy said.

"I'm heading back in," Conner said.

"Leave the door open so I don't have to buzz upstairs again. They're getting cranky up there. I'll be back in five."

"Here's our chance," I whispered. We all moved to the black door.

"Let me go first," Jordan said. We followed her up a flight of stairs. The carpet on the stairs was worn-out, and it seemed like every other stair creaked. We went up another flight of stairs and then down a gloomy hallway lit with a solitary naked lightbulb hanging from the ceiling. We could hear music coming through a doorway at the end of the hall. We also heard footsteps coming up the stairs.

"In here!" I beckoned Lily and Jordan into a small room, and we closed the door. We waited for the footsteps to go past us. Ruff started sniffing around. "Please be quiet, please be quiet," I silently willed Ruff not to make any sudden dog noises. But he just kept sniffing. He nudged Lily over, and his nose went right for a small hole in the wall.

"Ruff! Over here!" I whispered. I pulled a dried-liver treat out of my pocket and lured him over to the corner. Then I got down on all fours and peeked through the hole. It looked right into the big room, but it was way too low to see anything except feet and legs. But two feet higher there was a wide crack that made quite a handy portal into the other room. They were all there: Nina; James; Ms. Murdoch; her brother, Conner; and about six other people. Each person—except Conner Murdoch—was at an easel. To the unsuspecting eye, it might look like some kind of hip art jam, with a bunch of artists hanging out together and making art to loud music. But no one here looked like they were having fun. In fact, they all looked tortured.

I could see why.

Mimi Hansen came into view. She walked by each easel. "Hmm . . . this one might work. And this one works. Very Hansen. Yes, that's good. Very Hansen. Yes, yes. That's so Hansen!" She clapped her hands to get their attention, just like she was a first-grade teacher. Maybe we could see only part of her through the hole, but her voice was coming through loud and clear.

"Listen up, people. It's only a week until the Honcho auction. I need each of you to finish one more painting by Wednesday. There are only two here tonight that are ready for me to sign," she said. "You really need to crank it up." She walked over to a painting James was doing. "I'm ready to sign this one." She elbowed James out of the way.

"It's not actually finished," he said.

"I say it is finished, and that means it's finished," Mimi hissed. "You need to start another painting. Now!"

"She's so mean. Oops. Sorry!" Lily grimaced toward Jordan.

"It's okay," Jordan whispered back.

Mimi took the painting from James's easel and brought it over to a large worktable. Mr. Snotty Art Guy was back in the room now. He photographed the painting and wrote something down in a ledger.

"Listen up, people!" Mimi called to the room. She turned down the music on the boom box. "You can take a break in ten. But it looks like it will be a long night."

Just then Jordan's cell phone rang. Oops, she mouthed. Lily and I glared at her.

"Were you expecting anyone else?" I heard Mimi ask.

Jordan sighed and climbed out of the closet. We peered out the door as she walked down the hall toward the studio and Mimi Hansen.

"Hello, Mother," Jordan said.

"Jordan! What are you doing here? You know I must work in private," Mimi said. That was a hoot, since she certainly wasn't working—and there were nine people who were.

"Don't worry, Mother. I'm not here to bother you. I just need some cash," Jordan said. She held out her hand, palm up, with the air of a bored pampered teenager.

Hmm . . . not bad, Jordan, I thought. Maybe she could join the Lily Shannon Acting Troupe.

"Come on! Let's get out of here!" I carried Ruff and led Lily out of the closet, down the hall, back down two flights of stairs, and out onto First Avenue.

CHAPTER 24

"DO YOU HAVE a plan?" Lily asked.

"My plan is gadgets. We need some gadgets," I said. Ruff barked. "Thank you for not doing that inside," I added, nuzzling my nose into his neck.

We went up to our apartment and grabbed Mom's digital camera. Mom needed it for her work at the magazine, and she had made it very clear that I was not supposed to touch it. But these were extraordinary circumstances. On second thought, a video camera would be even better. I opened Owen's office. He'd purposefully left all his high-tech gear at home so he could "get back to nature" on his trip. I didn't think he'd mind if I borrowed his digital video camera. Or one of his digital video cameras, I should say. I had my choice of four. "Sweet!" I said, holding up a black camera as small as a credit card.

"Cool!" Lily said. "I didn't even know they made them that small."

"Here, you can use this one," I said. I handed her another camera that was about the size of a TV remote control.

"Okay, I'll use this huge one. But what am I doing with it?" Lily asked.

"We need to prove that Mimi Hansen is a big fat fake," I said. "No one will believe us. But if we can get some pictures of her factory, then maybe people will stop worshiping her."

"Wow! We solved our first case!" Lily said. We got on the elevator to go downstairs.

"Not yet. We know the answer to one part. But we still don't know who was stealing the paintings," I said.

"I thought it was Mr. Bike Messenger Guy," Lily said. "Ms. Murdoch's brother."

"I'm not so sure. I still think he can't be trusted, but I'm not sure how he fits in. What would his motive be?"

"Money? That's usually a pretty good motive," Lily said.

She had a point. But something still didn't seem quite right.

Our timing was perfect. We reached the black door to The Factory just as a couple of the guys we'd seen upstairs were heading back in. Their break must be over. I grabbed the door before it closed completely. We waited until the footsteps heading upstairs got softer and faded. We tiptoed up the stairs and back into the little closet. Drat! I was so used to taking Ruff everywhere that I still had him with me. The little guy was being especially mellow, as if he was trying to prove his worthiness for undercover work.

"Let's see if this works," I said. I put the viewfinder of the camera right up to the peephole and started videotaping.

"Darn!" I had to suppress a laugh when I passed it to Lily to take a look. The camera had captured James's dreadlocks and half of Ms. Murdoch. "I don't suppose Mimi will be crouching down so I can get her head into a shot, will she?" I whispered. "Because this isn't the kind of video that makes good TV."

"I'll take care of it," Lily said. "But you have to give me the little cute camera. I've had enough of this monster."

Lily handed over the comparatively huge three-inch camera, and I reluctantly gave her the teensy tiny one. She looked at me intensely. "On second thought," she whispered, "this is your gig." She handed the miniature video camera back to me.

"Huh?" Oops. I hope I didn't say that too loudly. But as it turns out, we could probably be talking in normal voices and no one in The Factory would be able to hear us. Lily crossed her arms and sighed as if exasperated with me. "It's time, Hannah my dear, for you to go onstage. Now."

I knew she was right. Not about me acting, but about me getting to the bottom of this. If there was a bottom to be found, I was the one who was going to find it, and if I was lucky, I wouldn't end up on my own bottom. I put some Burt's Bees lip balm on my lips and did a silent smacking. I did a quick finger comb of my hair and then flipped it over my shoulder in what I hoped was a dramatic manner.

"Perfect!" Lily crooned. "Now go break a leg. But don't really break a leg or trip or do anything klutzy." Her confidence in me seemed to be waning.

She gently shoved me out of the closet and into the hallway. I took a deep breath and barged right through the door of The Factory. It was a showstopping entrance, if I do say so myself, yet no one even noticed me. The music was still loud, and all the artists were intensely working at their easels. Mimi was intently text messaging on her cell phone. Excellent. I could get some good shots before they noticed me.

I cupped Owen's tiny digital camera in the palm of my hand and started filming.

"Excuse me!" I called over the music. I waved my hands slowly over my head to get their attention. It was hard not to smile at my improvisational skills, since the hand-waving gesture was just to get some more video shots.

Mimi Hansen motioned for someone to turn down the music.

"You again! You seem to frequently appear in the wrong places," she said. "And this time, you have the wrong floor. This is a private workspace. Please leave."

"I'm sorry. I need help," I said. "I'm trying to find Nina Krimmel."

"Hannah?" Nina came out from behind an easel. "What are you doing here? How did you find me?" She turned to Mimi. "No one knew I was here. I didn't tell anyone, really."

Geesh. I hated to see Nina grovel.

"Nina!" I ran over to her. But I didn't take the most

direct route. I wove my way through the room, passing paintings with the camera still cupped in my hand. "I'm so sorry," I said when I got to Nina. "I need your help. It's an emergency," she said.

"What's wrong? Are you okay? Is Maggie okay?" Nina looked genuinely worried. I must be pretty good at this acting thing.

"Yes! It's Maggie. AND Lily. And Billy Bob and Bobbie Joe, too," I said. Hey, I couldn't be expected to be totally original with names when I was improvising.

Nina looked at me like, *Huh, what the heck are you talking about?*

"You can't let outsiders into The Factory!" Mimi bellowed. "I don't know who this girl is or how she found you, but I can assure you that you are no longer creating Mimi Hansen art. Nor will you be paid for this evening's work."

"Oh, who cares!" Nina snapped. "Some things are more important than Mimi Hansen!"

"Right on, Nina!" I said. Oops. I forgot I was in the middle of an "emergency." I moved back into my sniveling role. "Nina, please, we need to go now." I started marching out of the workroom as if on a mission, but I wanted to get more video shots. The inspiring words of my acting coach, the great Lily Shannon, seeped into my head: *Break a leg. But don't really break a leg or trip or do anything klutzy.*

So I tripped.

CHAPTER 25

WHILE DOWN ON all fours, I readjusted the camera in my hand and figured out how to stand back up while getting some more video.

"Oh, oh, oh! I'm so sorry. I'm so embarrassed. I just am just so worried about Bobbie Bill and Billy Joel," I said, all weepy.

"Don't you mean Billy Bob and Bobbie Joe?" Conner Murdoch asked.

"Give her a break!" Nina snapped. "Can't you see how upset she is? We need to get out of here. Come on, Hannah. We've got to get to Billy Joel and Billy Bob."

"Billy Bob and Bobbie Joe," Conner called after us.

"Whatever," I said.

Nina and I made a run for it.

Lily and Ruff met us in the hallway, and we charged down the two flights of stairs and out onto the sidewalk.

"Come on! Back to our apartment," I said.

*

We started sprinting. "You'd better tell me that everyone is okay," Nina panted.

"Mom and I are fine. We just wanted to get you out of there before anything happens," I said. "Sorry if I scared you too much."

"You were brilliant!" Lily said. "You've learned a lot from me, I must say."

"You had me going at first. Billy Bob and Bobbie Joe was a little over-the-top, but it got my attention," Nina said. "When we get upstairs, we're calling Maggie, and then you're telling both of us what's going on."

"I'm sorry if we blew it for you, Nina, but we wanted to get you out of there," I said.

"Why? Nothing dangerous was going on. I mean, I'm not proud of the fact that I've been painting pieces for Mimi Hansen to pass off as her own. But it wasn't like I was her prisoner or anything."

"I wanted you out because we took some video of what was going on inside The Factory," I said. "I'm going to call Mom and ask her to see if Mary Perez wants to look at it."

We got off the elevator, and I fumbled for the keys to the apartment.

"I don't know if it's exactly newsworthy that we're painting for someone else," Nina said. "It's not even illegal."

"It should be illegal!" I cried. "She's a big fake. It's fraud. People are paying her for things she didn't create. You're an artist, Nina! You deserve to have your name on your work, and you deserve recognition for your work. I can't stand Mimi Hansen getting all the credit for what other people have done."

"She won't be getting credit for long," a man's voice said.

Conner Murdoch was in the hallway, right behind us.

"I'll take that video you took while you were so concerned about your Billy Bob," Conner said.

"I don't know what you're talking about," Lily claimed. "Can't you see we're having a family emergency?"

"Get off it." Conner sneered. He pulled something from his bag. "Here, doggy. Come and get it." Ruff leaped toward whatever was inside the brown wrapper, and in one smooth motion Conner scooped up the pup and backed away from us.

"Give me your camera, and I'll give you the mutt."

"Ruff!" I lunged toward Conner, but he stuffed Ruff into his bag.

"Perhaps you didn't hear me. You give me the camera; I give you the dog."

"Why are you protecting Mimi Hansen? You should want her to be exposed for the fake she is," I said, trying to not let a begging tone enter my voice. "Your own sister is being used."

"I'm not protecting Mimi anymore," he said with a hint of disgust, as if I was a total idiot for even thinking that.

"Conner, really, this is a bit extreme. I'm not sure yet if it's funny or embarrassing," Nina said. "For you, that is." He dropped Ruff and left abruptly.

CHAPTER 26

"I NEED TO get to Wired. I'm working the late shift tonight," Nina said. "What should I tell Maggie when I get there?"

"Never mind. I'm here," Mom called from the doorway of the apartment. "I couldn't get Hannah to answer her cell phone. I called you, Nina, to check on Hannah, but you didn't answer, either. I called the apartment and still no answer. Is everything okay?"

"The girls can explain. I really better get to work," Nina said. "I lost one job tonight. I can't afford to lose the other." I winced when she said that. "I'm kidding, Hannah. I hated working for Mimi. You know that," she said, giving me a quick hug before she left the apartment.

We filled Mom in on The Factory and who was there. "Look, we can show you," Lily said. We went to the computer and downloaded the video from Owen's camera.

"So the old marketing wizard runs an art factory, and then just puts her signature on other people's work?" Mom said. "It makes perfect sense. There was always something so artificial about the way Mimi talked about art. It didn't seem possible that one person could do so many paintings, let alone have such a wide variety of art styles."

"I'm pretty sure there's more to the story," I said. "I think Mimi arranged the thefts."

"This would be a great story for Mary Perez," Mom said.

"We could take her over to The Factory tonight, and she could pin down Mimi," I said.

Mary was at our apartment in twelve minutes. After she'd watched the video, we showed her the door to The Factory across the street. "Maybe I can get our own news crew in there tonight," she said. "Or maybe I need to be more covert. I think I'll go interview Mimi off camera."

"Good luck getting her to talk if there isn't a camera on her face," I said.

Lily and I stayed out on the balcony and watched Mary cross First Avenue. Lily had the binoculars focused toward The Factory door.

"It looks like something is up in the world of purple and black," Lily said.

Conner Murdoch and his bike were back at The Factory.

"What are you doing carrying the dog?" Lily panted as we ran out of Belltown Towers and onto the sidewalk.

"Well, I couldn't leave him in Owen's apartment. We're going to have to keep him with us," I said.

We were running without a plan. We crossed the street and headed toward the black door to The Factory.

"Aaarrrgggh!" Wouldn't you know it? I tripped again. I went sprawling down on the sidewalk. Ruff escaped from my arms.

"Ruff! Come!" I called as I tried to get up with a little bit of dignity.

Conner Murdoch was coming out the door with a rectangular flat package in his arms. He didn't even look in our direction. He just jumped on his bike and started pedaling.

Only he had a hitchhiker.

"Off! Get off!" he yelled.

But Ruff had gotten hold of his left sock, and it didn't look like the little terrier had any intention of letting go. Conner tried to pedal a few times.

Ruff clenched his little teeth tightly on Conner's sock. There's no way that terrier was going to let go. Ruff just went around and around while Conner tried to pedal.

Crash!

Ruff was still hanging on.

Conner jumped off his bike and started running.

Ruff hung on.

Conner and Ruff made it only a few steps.

"Have a nice trip!" a voice called out. Suddenly Jordan Walsh was back in the action, sticking her leg out as if she were a third-grade bully.

"Conner!" Ms. Murdoch exclaimed as he tumbled to the ground. Mimi Hansen, Mary Perez, Mr. Snotty Art Guy, and James were right behind her. Ruff escaped the crowd and ran back to me.

"You again," Mr. Snotty Art Guy sneered his greeting to me.

"Jordan!" Mimi said. "I thought your father was picking you up."

"He's still running late," Jordan said in a somewhat blasè voice. "Am I interrupting something?"

"Conner, why did you take one of my paintings?" Ms. Murdoch asked her brother, looking down at the canvas that was peeking out from under the Kraft paper wrapping.

"That wasn't in the plans!" Mimi said, admonishing Conner. "Did you know about this?" She turned to Mr. Snotty Art Guy, who just shook his head.

"I did it for you," Conner said quietly to his sister. "I don't want you involved in any of this."

Mary Perez was looking from Mimi to Conner, who was still on the ground, as if deciding who to go after. I couldn't help myself. I had to butt in.

"The plans? You mean you knew what was going on all along? I knew it! You were stealing your own paintings!" I stared at Mimi. She didn't say anything. "Wait! Let me correct that. You were hiring people to create paintings that you passed off as your own, and then you tried to steal them?"

"Brilliant bit of publicity, wasn't it?" Conner Murdoch said, standing up and brushing himself off.

Mimi, the queen of publicity and TV interviews, seemed absolutely speechless now. Then she cleared her throat. "I'm sure I don't know what you're talking about," she said. "I'm ready to talk on TV now," she said to Mary. "I want to do all I can to help you break this story to get to the bottom of who was stealing Mimi Hansen paintings." She looked poised for a full TV interview now. You had to give her credit, she really recovered her public persona quickly.

"I have a few questions to ask you and the others before I ask you to comment on camera," Mary said. "Perhaps we could start upstairs with the artists' help in identifying their work."

"I would like to identify my work," James said.

"Conner, I don't know what's going on," Ms. Murdoch said to her brother. "But I think I'll go stand behind my work right now." She went upstairs, too.

"I have an idea how your mom can stand behind the artists' work—the real artists' work," I said to Jordan.

I headed upstairs with Jordan and the others. I figured if the proposal came from Mimi's daughter, and in front of witnesses, she'd have a harder time saying no. By the time I had explained it all to her, Jordan had a big smile on her face. This time, I could tell that it was sincere.

CHAPTER 27

AND THAT'S HOW we all ended up here at the Fairmont Olympic Hotel. Lily, Mom, Nina, James, Ms. Murdoch, Jordan Walsh, Mary Perez, and me—all at our own table at the Honcho auction. Jordan even had her limousine pick us up for the ride over.

Sure, our table is in the back of the room close to the kitchen, but just getting in the door is $250 a head. We were here compliments of Mimi Hansen. That's right. Mimi Hansen bought us tickets—$2,000 for our seats—to the auction. And the best was yet to come.

"What did we miss?" Lily asked when she and Jordan got back from the bathroom.

"Let's see . . . a dinner for two on a sailboat in Shilshole Bay Marina for twelve hundred and fifty dollars—and the boat isn't even going anywhere. A weekend at Whistler for four thousand fifty dollars. A glass bowl by one of Dale Chihuly's students for twelve thousand." I rattled off the prices. Mom and I were keeping track of each item in the hefty program.

"Are you kidding? Twelve grand for a bowl? I'd be afraid to eat my Frosted Mini-Wheats in a bowl that cost that much," Lily said.

"Don't worry," Jordan said. "You didn't buy it."

"You guys! This is the best part coming up," I said. I looked over at Nina and James. "I mean, this is the *second* best part coming up."

The tuxedoed auctioneer onstage boomed, "Ladies and gentlemen, this brings us to the canine portion of our evening, beginning with Willow!" A beautiful Weimaraner with clear blue eyes came onstage, accompanied by a woman in a sparkling gray gown that complemented Willow's coat. The dog stayed calm despite the applause. Bidding began at $1,500 and didn't stop until $8,000.

"I want to make sure Walker goes to a good home," I said, pointing out an entry in the program.

Walker came out onstage with a black velvet bow tie. "And here he is. A one hundred percent Shelter Special. All the dog you need in one package," the auctioneer said. "Let's start the bidding at one hundred dollars." That seemed a little insulting to Walker, who was an adorable medium-size mutt with a golden coat and white paws. Soon I had new respect for these Honcho folks, because there was passionate bidding for Walker. He seemed to know all the excitement was for him, because when bidding topped out at $9,500, he started barking.

Dorothy Powers was up onstage now. "It is my pleasure

to introduce to you Mimi Hansen." Mimi, resplendent in a backless shimmering lavender gown and high-rise heels, hugged Dorothy as the crowd clapped enthusiastically.

"At this time, I'd like to unveil some of the greatest talent in art today," Mimi began. One of the spotlights hit our table as Mimi continued: "Nina Krimmel, Shelley Murdoch, and James Farnsworth. Tonight you have the rare opportunity to bid on these artists' work and then watch as they sign their work in front of you." The applause was deafening.

"I'm so nervous," Nina said. "What if no one bids?"

She needn't have worried. Bidding was fast and high, with each painting going for at least $15,000, including the one by Ms. Murdoch that Conner had attempted to steal and return to his sister. Everyone in the crowd rose to their feet as the artists from our table worked their way up to the stage to sign their paintings. Mimi had promised to pay each of them half of what each painting sold for as her "donation to the arts." Mom said it was guilt money, but Nina said it seemed cleaner to her than the $300 she would have gotten from Mimi for working at The Factory.

The artists working at The Factory had ended up on the Channel 4 News last weekend, and they'd stayed in the news all week. However, Mimi still emerged as the star in the public's eyes. She claimed the artists were working on pieces she'd commissioned for the auction and that there was no question that they would receive full credit for their work. That took care of the unsigned paintings, but she hadn't come up with a good scheme for the ones she'd actually signed. Mr. Chomsky, our upstairs neighbor, had been working on his own to trace who had actually created the paintings Mimi Hansen had claimed—and sold—as her own.

Speaking of Mr. Chomsky, I needed to get some footage of this part of the auction for him. Even with all the excitement of the auction and solving the Mimi mystery, he still wouldn't leave his apartment.

Conspicuously absent from this Mimi Hansen-loving crowd were Conner Murdoch and Mr. Snotty Art Guy. Conner had been delivering packages on the side to Mr. Chomsky. That turned out to be completely unrelated to the work he was doing for Mimi Hansen. But Conner admitted that he'd delivered the blank canvas to Dorothy Powers as an attempt to show Mimi that she needed to watch out or he'd leak it to the press that she was orchestrating all the thefts, with his help and a gallery insider (Mr. Snotty Art Guy). Mary Perez was going to break that story after the auction.

It was all coming together quite nicely, I thought as I put Owen's tiny video camera away.

"Hannah, this was all such a great idea," Nina said. "I wish I could thank you."

"I think you've come up with a pretty decent way to help us out," Mom said. She passed her phone to me so I could read her text message: 436 Portage Bay, Dock 3.

"What's that?" I asked.

"That's our next address," Mom said. "Thanks to a customer at Wired that Nina met."

"It doesn't look like a real address to me."

"I assure you that it's quite real. In fact, I predict you'll be so happy living there you'll be walking on water," she said.

"Huh?"

"And sleeping on water," she added.

"Again, I say: Huh?"

"Oh brother, Hannah. You can put together all kinds of clues for this Mimi Hansen publicity stunt and art heist, and yet you can't read your own mother. Maggie is practically spoon-feeding clues to you. Walking on water. Portage Bay. Dock," Lily said. "You're going to be living . . ."

". . . on a houseboat!" I finished for her.

"Finally," Lily said with a big sigh. "For a smart girl, you can be kind of slow."

I decided to ignore Lily.

"Really, Mom? We're living on a houseboat?"

"Really, Hannah. We're going to live on Jake Heard's houseboat on Lake Washington."

"We're going to live on a houseboat!" I yelped.

"It will be wonderfully quiet," Mom said wistfully.

"I just hope it's not too dull," I said.

"I bet nothing strange ever happens on the tranquil waters of Lake Washington," Lily said.

BOOK TWO

HANNAH WEST
in
DEEP WATER

CHAPTER 1

"I CAN'T BELIEVE you get to live here," Lily said from the backseat. "This is totally cool."

"Lucky for you that I still let you be my friend," I said. I was secretly pleased that Lily sounded impressed. Mom and I might be only temporary residents on Portage Bay, but you have to admit that it's a pretty sweet deal to get to live on a houseboat.

"There's the entrance to our dock," Mom said, pointing to a sidewalk that led toward Lake Washington. She pulled our battered old Honda Civic into a spot across the street. "It's a bit hidden from the street, but it's always easy to spot because of the mailboxes."

"Even our mailboxes are cool," I said smugly to Lily. I never gave much thought to mailboxes before except when I'd seen an occasional one shaped like Snoopy's dog house or with a propeller to look like an airplane or something. The Portage Bay dock mailboxes were the traditional metal style, but each had a fresh coat of paint in the solid, bright colors of blue, green, and white. Purple, red, and white flowers grew below the mailboxes, and even more bright blooms cascaded out of baskets positioned around the mailbox platform.

"It's just like *Sleepless in Seattle*," Lily said. "This is so exciting!"

It really was like *Sleepless in Seattle*, the 1990s movie with Tom Hanks and Meg Ryan. Much of the movie was set on a houseboat, giving the rest of the world the cockamamie idea that if you live in Seattle you could easily choose—and afford—to live on a houseboat. Actually, there are 570,000 people in Seattle and 1.8 million people in the county, but only five-hundred-some houseboats. That means only . . . well, you get the idea.

We stepped out of the car and into the rain. Now, I don't want you to get the wrong idea about Seattle. Despite its reputation as the Rainy City, Seattle is actually pretty sunny in the summer. Except for today, that is. Just figures that a nonstop drizzle fell from the sky to greet me on my first day as a houseboat resident. I was wearing long pants for the first time in two months.

"Maggie! There you are!" Rushing toward us came a gray-haired and bearded man pulling a rolling suitcase with one hand and holding an apricot-colored dog on a leash with the other.

"Hi, Jake. Are you leaving already?" Mom said.

"I'm so sorry. In the rush to get out of town I completely forgot to call and tell you that Heather wanted to get to the airport early. There's a new day spa there, and she needs a pedicure before we get on our flight," he said.

Lily and I rolled our eyes at each other. This guy was making it sound like a medical emergency when in fact his girlfriend just wanted to get her toenails painted before she went to France. He fumbled in his shoulder bag and jangled things around until he pulled out a set of keys and handed them to Mom. "I left a notebook of information on the desk for you and Hannah." He looked at Lily when he said my name. Lily doesn't look like blond, curly-haired Maggie West, but she's definitely a closer match to my mom than I am with my straight black hair, olive skin, and brown, almond-shaped eyes.

"That's me," I said, before Jake could embarrass himself by assuming that the Chinese girl couldn't be Maggie's daughter. "I'm Hannah, and this is my friend, Lily. And you must be Mango!" I bent down to meet Jake's apricot-colored dog.

"I'm going to miss Mango so much," Jake said, rather reluctantly handing the leash over to me. Jake looked seriously stressed about leaving his dog, which I fully expected based on the lengthy e-mail messages he'd sent Mom over the past few weeks. Jake wanted to be sure we knew all about labradoodles. That's right: labradoodles. You see, Mango is half Labrador retriever and half Standard poodle. But don't go thinking of him as a mutt, because these lab and poodle mixes are bred on purpose. In fact, it seemed as if labradoodles were the hot dogs of the year in Seattle. The poodle in them meant that they didn't shed, making them good for people with dog allergies. The Labrador in them assured that they'd be gentle, friendly, and loyal.

"Maggie, listen," Jake went on, "there's a film crew that's going to be here this week. I'm assured it's no big deal, but I thought I should warn you."

"Film crew? For a movie? Anyone famous going to be here?" Lily piped in. She's an actress impatiently waiting for her big break.

"What? Famous? Oh, the film. I don't know," Jake said distractedly. "It's a movie or something for a cable-TV channel."

I could tell that Lily was thinking "cable-TV channel" could be the big time, especially if it was HBO or Showtime. I didn't want to point out that it could also be one of those public access channels, or maybe instead of a movie it was a program on saving salmon or the merits of proper dental hygiene.

A yellow cab pulled up to the curb and honked. A tall woman with high strappy sandals that made her even taller got out of the backseat and motioned impatiently toward us. Jake's face literally melted, going from stressed out to all soft and lovey-dovey when he saw her.

"There's Heather. I need to go." He hugged Mango again. "Thanks for everything, Maggie. Oh, one last thing." He pulled an envelope out of his bag and handed it to Mom. I was betting it was more instructions on caring for Mango. "I'm not sure how much the filming will disrupt things. But just in case it inconveniences you, here's a little something to make up for it."

"Thank you, but that's really not necessary," Mom began, but Jake was already rushing over to the cab. I snatched the envelope from Mom and took a quick look inside to find a restaurant gift certificate. Mom might be too polite to look inside in front of him, but it didn't matter anyway, because Jake had eyes only for Heather. He gave her a quick kiss. I swear she rolled her eyes as he reached up and his lips made contact with her cheek. He was at least a half foot shorter than his girlfriend. I'm all for tall women and short men getting together with confidence, but this couple looked a bit cartoonish. Jake has that Mr. Northwest look— the kind of older guy who buys all his clothes at REI and hikes year-round and thinks it's acceptable to wear socks with hiking sandals. His girlfriend looked as if she'd send a servant outside to bend over to pick up the newspaper in the morning.

"We're going to be late," she snapped, moving away from him. "Just let the house sitters take care of everything." She said "house sitters" so that it sounded like "low-life servants."

"I'm so sorry. I'll make it up to you," Jake said, following her into the backseat of the taxi.

We watched as the taxi drove off, and then we headed toward the houseboat.

"Poor Jake. I hope they'll still be together after nine weeks in Europe," Mom said.

"I know what you mea—"

Splat! I slipped on the dock and fell flat on my butt. "Vincent! Pollock!" I cried, as the plastic bag I'd carried swooped out of my grasp.

Plop. It fell into the water.

Mango barked.

"No, Mango! No!" I cried.

And then . . . a much bigger *plop.*

CHAPTER 2

"MANGO, NO!" I cried, struggling to get up. "If he bites that plastic bag, it's all over for Vincent and Pollock," I whined as I watched him dog paddle toward the Ziploc bag that was serving as temporary transportation for my two goldfish.

"Here, Mango! Here, boy!" Mom joined me at the very edge of the dock, calling out to the dog, who was now in full fetch mode. He is, after all, half Labrador retriever. Then again, he's also half poodle, which might mean he'd decide to obey Mom's command and swim back to us.

Plop. Plop-plop.

A fluorescent green tennis ball landed in the water to the left of Mango's head. Two more tennis balls followed in quick succession.

"Get the ball, Mango," a small older woman instructed as she walked toward us. Obligingly, Mango turned his course toward the ball, intent on his mission.

"Good boy! Keep going!" Lily, Mom, and I cheered him on as if his task was the most difficult in the world. Mango glided through the water, bringing the tennis ball back to the edge of the dock. The woman bent over to get it from him and to scratch him behind the ears. "Good boy! Now get the other ones! Get them!" she commanded.

"I didn't really need to tell him to get the other balls. He's obsessed with tennis balls, and he won't stop until he gets them all," she told us. "Here, you can toss this one again if he gets the other two before I get back." She handed me the soggy green ball and headed into a white houseboat with green trim. She came back out with a net and a paddle. "Keep telling him he's a good boy. I'll get your package. What's in it, by the way?" She kept talking while she effortlessly lifted a kayak off the dock, lowered it into the water, and then slipped inside and pushed herself off from the dock.

"My goldfish. They're in a plastic bag," I said, pointing. "Do you see them? It kind of looks like a bubble. Oh, good dog, Mango." I accepted the third soggy tennis ball from him and then hurled it out farther into the water, just to make sure he'd stay occupied until Vincent and Pollock got safely back.

"Got it!" the woman called from the kayak. "Or should I say, 'got them'? Because it looks like there are two perfectly fine goldfish inside here."

"Thank you so much!" I was practically shrieking with happiness. When you're technically homeless like Mom and me, you get pretty attached to the few things that you have. And I'm terribly attached to my two goldfish named after Vincent van Gogh and Jackson Pollock, two of my all-time-favorite artists. My fish rescuer pulled her kayak up to the dock and handed my pets to me. I kissed the plastic bag, wishing once again that they were the kind of pets you could pet and nuzzle. Right then Mango, a big bundle in need of some grateful nuzzling, returned to the dock, too.

"Lily, will you hold my boys?" I handed the fish to her so I could bend down and get the ball from Mango. I clumsily helped him get back up on the dock, a chore that left me almost as wet as the shaggy, soaked dog. He tried to lick the water off me, which made me laugh so hard that he easily knocked me over. While I was being a total dog-loving klutz, the woman had somehow gotten herself and her kayak out of the water without so much as a drop of water getting on her.

"Thank you so much for your help," Mom said to the woman. "I'm afraid we made a bit bigger splash than I'd hoped for when we arrived."

"Don't worry about it," the mystery woman said. "Mango was just doing his job. It's what he was bred to do. Or at least, it's what half of him was bred to do. Jake gave me those tennis balls when I was dog-sitting Mango."

"They certainly came in handy today," I said. "I really want to thank you for saving Vincent and Pollock."

"Vincent and Pollock? What great names. Makes me

think of two of my favorite artists," she said. "Are you by chance an art lover?"

"I am," I said.

"It's not often that I meet a teenager who likes my two favorite artists," she said.

I didn't say anything because I was busy thinking how much I liked being called a teenager, which I'm not. Not yet. I'm still twelve.

"She's an artist, too," Lily piped in. "I'm her agent."

"And I'm her mother," Mom said. "Alice, I'd like you to meet my daughter, Hannah West, and her friend, Lily Shannon. Girls, this is Alice Campbell. Jake introduced me to her the first time I came to see him. He said that anything we want to know, we can just ask Alice."

Alice smiled and held her hand out to shake. Her eyes twinkled as she looked directly at me. She looked Japanese, but I wasn't sure. There wasn't any clue in her name. Then again, there isn't any real clue in my name that I'm Chinese, unless you associate my middle name, Jade, with China (which is exactly why it's my middle name).

"I'm also a dog walker," I said.

I handed her my card, which unfortunately was a little soggy:

Hannah J. West

Pet Sitter, Dog Walker,
Plant Waterer, and
all around Errand Girl

235-6628

"Delightful! Nice to meet you, too, Lily," she said, shaking Lily's hand.

I liked Alice Campbell immediately. Not only had she saved my fish, but she wasn't treating us like little kids.

"Welcome to the Portage Bay Floating Home Association," Alice said. "Maggie, I'm betting that what Jake really said is that I'm president of our little association here. Please don't hesitate to ask if you need anything. You'll find that everyone on this particular dock is extremely friendly. We all look out for one another. Your next-door neighbors, Mike and Betsy, are on vacation right now. And so is Patrick down on this end. But everyone else is around and excited to meet you. I'd love to invite you in for tea, but I'm sure you want to get settled."

"Hannah hasn't even seen the inside of the houseboat yet," Mom said.

"You'll love it, I'm sure. Now, I hate to be bossy," Alice

continued in a tone of voice that people use when they say that they hate to be bossy, but then they act bossy anyway. "But before you leave, you need to bring Mango over to my porch so we can rinse him off. In fact, we'll give him a full bath. Now, now, now. I insist." I could tell there was no getting Mango out of this bath.

"Didn't he just have a bath in the lake?" Lily asked.

"No!" Alice said sharply. "He must be thoroughly cleaned if he gets lake water on him. Jake may have neglected to tell you that, but I assure you, it's terribly important. Hannah, please promise me that you'll clean Mango thoroughly if he gets any lake water on him."

"Um, okay," I said, a bit confused about the sudden urgency in her voice.

"In fact, I encourage you to take a shower since he shook water all over you, too," she said. I gave her a look that must have conveyed what was going through my head: Are you crazy? It's just a little bit of water. She seemed to read my mind.

"Well, at least you should all wash your hands. Now, let's get this dog hosed off," she said. There didn't seem to be any question that Mango was getting a full dockside scrub down, complete with some lavender-scented Buddy Wash dog soap.

"Do you have a dog?" I asked Alice.

"Oh, no," she said, still intently scrubbing and rinsing Mango.

"I was just wondering why you have dog soap handy," I said.

"Sometimes I give Mango a bath. Jake's good about rinsing him off after muddy walks or when he gets in the water here, but I think he needs a little more."

It seemed a little presumptuous for someone to give someone else's dog a bath, but I was new here. Maybe it was the kind of place where bathing a dog is like baking brownies to show your neighbors you like them. Or maybe Alice was an obsessive clean freak and people happily left the pet bathing in her capable hands. It was curious but didn't really matter. I just wanted to get this dog clean and toweled off so I could see our new house.

Okay, okay. It's not really "our" house. And I'm not really homeless, either. Although technically I don't have a permanent address. Don't get all panicky like we're cagey criminals or in the witness protection program or something. We're professional house sitters, which sounds glamorous, but it means that we pack up and move every couple of weeks. This was our first time house-sitting in a houseboat, or a "floating home" as those in the know say. It was going to feel more like being on vacation than house-sitting. It was an extra bonus that the house came with a dog. I've done tons of dog walking before, but never round-the-clock doggy duty.

After two rounds of sudsing and three rinses, Alice deemed Mango clean and ready to go. Finally! "Let's go home, boy," I said, and Lily, Mom, and I followed Mango down the dock. I'd been so busy worrying about Vincent, Pollock, and Mango that I hadn't really looked at the houseboats on our L-shaped dock. Each house was painted a fresh, warm color—vibrant blue, true red, a deep gray that somehow looked cheery—or a bright white. Windows and trim were painted a distinctly contrasting color, giving each little house a crisp, clean look. Window boxes and terra-cotta planters overflowed with flowers blooming in reds, purples, blues, hot pinks, and whites. I felt as if I was in a poster-sized print of a charming alley in a European village. Everything was fresh and gorgeous, complemented by the gentle lapping sound of the water under the dock. Mom had told me that Jake's cottage had the best spot on the dock, since it was at the very end of the "L" with water surrounding it on three sides. The house was blue with white-and-purple trim.

A rustling noise caught my attention just before I got to our entrance. I turned to look. Two people dressed head to toe in black rain gear scurried out from the cottage porch next door. Each black-hooded figure carried two large white buckets as they practically trotted back toward the street. Weird. Alice Campbell had just told us that our next-door neighbors were on vacation. Maybe people rich enough for houseboats get their houses cleaned even when they're not there.

*

"Welcome home!" Mom said as she opened the deep purple door of our houseboat. Her arms stretched wide. "Come inside and check it out!"

Mango obviously didn't need an invitation. He barreled past Mom and up the first two rungs of a ladder-style staircase that went up to a sleeping loft above. I heard a cat meow from the loft area. "That must be Hank," I said. Hank was Jake's cat. I'd already heard that Mango loved Hank, but the cat was not returning the sentiment.

"This is fabulous!" Lily gushed. I walked into a small kitchen that opened up to a light-filled living room with wall-to-wall windows. A deck wrapped around the north and east sides of the living room, making it seem as if the whole house was floating on Lake Washington. Wait. What am I saying? The whole house *was* floating on Lake Washington. It was so quiet this morning that I could hear the water lapping gently under the dock. I felt surrounded by water, but not wobbly like I would be if I were on a raft or in a boat. I explored every inch of the cottage, which didn't take long. The house was teensy tiny, but each room was perfect. My bedroom, which was really a guest room and office, had two windows facing toward the street, but with lots of water between me and the street. Bright red geraniums, purple petunias, and cascading vines with little white flowers spilled out of the window boxes. I could crank open the windows and smell the fresh lake water below. Bookshelves and wood file cabinets lined the walls.

A twin bed was shoved under a window, seeming more like a couch than a bed. But there was a laptop on the built-in desk and a small flat-screen TV on top of a dresser. Seemed like an ideal bedroom to me.

I followed Mom's voice up a ladder to the loft bedroom, which she obviously claimed as her own. She was the adult, after all. There was a big bed with a fluffy white down comforter and a half-dozen pillows piled on top. The room was open to the living room and windows below. It reminded me of a crow's nest on a big sailing ship.

Mango whined from down below. The ladder was too steep for him, a fact that obviously didn't escape the agile cat. Hank taunted him from above.

"It's okay, boy," I said, climbing back down. "Where do you sleep? Can you show me your bed?"

His ears perked up when I said "bed."

"Go to bed?" I asked hesitantly.

Mango trotted off to my bedroom and jumped up on the bed. He looked so proud of himself. "Good boy," I said, giving him a scratch behind the ears. "I think I have a bunk mate," I called up to Mom.

"Judging by all the cat hair, I think Hank likes to bunk up here," Mom said. "Jake said he left information in your room to let you know all you need for Mango. Have you come across it yet?"

I scanned the desk, looking for a note about dog care. Instead I found a two-inch-wide purple three-ring binder with a carefully made spine label that read MANGO CARE AND OTHER IMPORTANT INFORMATION. I pulled it out. The front of the notebook had a large color photograph of Mango, with the same words printed over the photo. Inside was a table of contents and carefully labeled sections that included "Feeding Mango," "Approved Training for Mango," and "Suggested Walking Routes for Mango." There were sections devoted to Mango's coat, teeth, and eyes, as well as emergency information about his veterinarian. The last section included general information about labradoodles, most of which he'd already e-mailed to us. An article on crossbreeding talked about other hot poodle mixes. It seems lots of people were intrigued with the idea of getting nonshedding dogs. Mix a cocker spaniel with a poodle and you get a cockapoo; take a miniature schnauzer and a poodle and you have a schnoodle; add a golden retriever to a poodle for a goldendoodle. The shih tzu and poodle mix had a couple of pretty funny combinations, too.

I looked at Mango. He looked like a regular, sweet dog to me. And right now he was looking at me as if I could be his favorite person in the world, if only I'd get on top of the bed with him and snuggle for a little while. "Later, boy," I said, giving him a big bear hug. He rewarded me with a moan of happiness.

"This is totally *Sleepless in Seattle*," Lily said from the living room. I headed back to the waterside room. I looked outside and saw a motorboat slowly pass by and then pick up speed. A sailboat with its mast down and its motor on puttered slowly past. I pulled out the camera my photography teacher had lent me and took a few shots. A few more boats passed by. One stopped, and I used the telephoto lens to zoom in. Two people wearing black rain gear were fiddling with something in the back. The taller one raised a white five-gallon bucket upside down over the side of the boat. The way he was flinging it around made it seem as if it was empty, sort of how those two people on the dock had been swinging empty white buckets. Those two people on the dock had also been wearing black. Hmmm . . . I zoomed in as much as I could, but it didn't do me much good because they weren't facing me. I clicked anyway. Darn! I was at the end of a twenty-four-exposure roll of film and I'd wasted at least six shots on those bucket people. The engine on the boat started up again, and they motored off. I sighed and rewound my film.

I loved this 35-millimeter manual Konica camera. It belonged to Greg, my photography teacher at Coyote Central, this cool middle school arts camp where I had a scholarship. I'd just finished a three-week photography class at Coyote, and he had let me experiment with a couple of his cameras. Until then I'd used only disposable or digital cameras, or those kind that auto-focus, auto-advance, and auto-everything. Photography was so much more fun with a camera that allows you to experiment with the focus and the aperture (which controls the amount of light that comes through). In drawing, sometimes I have to stop and let my eyes relax so I can see things fresh. I was finding that the same thing helped in photography, because otherwise it's too easy to get obsessed with looking at life through a lens. I closed my eyes and opened them to see if anything new appeared.

Nope. Just a bunch of boats. But soon a bit of a pattern emerged. Sailboats seemed to be heading one way; motorboats, the opposite direction.

"I'm guessing that the sailboats are heading out to the Puget Sound," Mom said, as she walked into the room and saw me looking at the boat traffic. "Remember how Robert used to rave about that?" There's a ship canal that links Lake Washington—where we were living—with Lake Union and the Puget Sound. It meant that boaters had the best of fresh water and salt water accessible to them. It didn't mean much to me, but grown-ups around here get all excited about the waterways. Robert, one of Mom's old bosses at MegaComp, used to go on and on about how "fabulous" it is to get in a boat on the far shore of Lake Washington in the morning and be up at an island in the Puget Sound in the afternoon.

"It was all he ever talked about," I added.

"Well, some people take their boating pretty seriously," she said. "And from what I hear, the motorboaters are even more into it than the sailboaters."

I let my mind wander to the idea that I was now living

in the midst of all these serious boaters. And even if we weren't going to be out there cruising with them, I was feeling pretty happy about the prospect of waking up on Lake Washington in the morning and going to sleep on Lake Washington at night. And I do mean on the lake.

CHAPTER 3

"WHOA! MY LEGS feel all wobbly and weird!" I said when I got back on solid land. I'd been on the houseboat for three hours and I already had my sea legs, I guess, because on land my legs felt like rubber. It took only a couple of steps before I was back to normal, though.

"Jake told me that it might feel weird to us for the first few seconds on land each day," Mom said. She and I were taking Mango on a walk around the Portage Bay neighborhood. Lily's parents had already picked her up, with a promise that she'd come back many, many times while we were living on the water. If word got out about where we were living, I could become quite popular, I bet. But, as always, we kept our house-sitting adventures hush-hush, particularly from the Seattle school district. Without a north Seattle address, I wouldn't be able to keep going to Cesar Chavez Middle School with Lily.

As we continued on our walk, Mom started pointing out street names. Ever since I was little, Mom had this annoying habit of reading street signs and addresses to me. It drove me crazy—and it still drives me crazy—but it has made it easier for me to find my way around. At a very early age, I learned that avenues ran north-south in Seattle and that streets ran east-west. It was pretty easy to figure out because the streets were set up like grids. Except in this neighborhood.

"None of the streets are straight! This is so confusing," I grumbled.

"Some of the streets follow the shoreline, but you'll get the hang of it pretty quickly," she said, pointing out that we were walking on Boyer Avenue. "This is the most important street for you to remember because—"

"Doughnuts straight ahead!" I cried.

"I was going to say because there's a bus stop in front of the Canal Market, but if it helps you get oriented by knowing they have doughnuts, then so be it," Mom said.

Mango was obviously a regular at the Canal Market. He knew just where to sit and wait while we went in to check out the doughnuts. He also seemed to know that no one exits the store without getting a dog treat. We left, and as we ate our doughnuts, we walked about nine blocks farther to a busy corner I recognized because of a Red Robin restaurant on the right. Our street intersected with Eastlake Avenue East, a street I knew well from the number 66.

"You're checking out the bus stops, aren't you?" Mom said.

"Yep."

"And I'm guessing that you've already memorized the routes and times by looking at the Metro schedule online?" she asked.

"Yep again. Except it's way better to actually see the bus stop than to just look on a map, especially when curvy streets are involved," I said. I was so relieved to see that I could walk straight down our street about twelve blocks to get on my favorite bus. Then it was just a couple miles south to get downtown or about five miles north to get to my old Maple Leaf neighborhood, where Lily still lived.

"We'll have to check out the number 25, too," Mom said.

"It comes every eighteen to twenty minutes during peak times, beginning at approximately six twenty-two A.M. To head downtown, I board on our side of the street, arriving downtown approximately thirteen minutes later. If I board on the other side of the street, I can get to the University of Washington, go shopping at University Village, or go to some neighborhood called Laurelhurst at any time after six thirty-one A.M.," I rattled off.

"Good to know," Mom said, looking suitably impressed.

"But be forewarned that midday the number 25 comes only once an hour," I said.

"You'll have to plan ahead," Mom said. "Or take another bus." She wrapped an arm around my shoulders, which I knew was her cornball-Mom way of saying that she was proud of my independence. At least that's what I choose to think it meant. We walked back on the opposite side of the street, passing our dock and continuing on past the sprawling St. Demetrios Greek Orthodox Church. Street after street of brick houses with pointy roofs and immaculate gardens welcomed us as we meandered past the Emerald City Yacht Club and the Montlake Community Center, where I first learned to play ultimate Frisbee, and into the arboretum. I've been to the Washington Park Arboretum (its official name) dozens of times on school field trips or with out-of-town relatives, but I'd never lived so close. I couldn't believe we could walk to so many things.

By the time we got back to our houseboat more than an hour later, the sun was out in full force. Mom and I decided to go out on the lake. Mango watched us from the living room window as we pushed off in Jake's double kayak.

"This is the life!" I said from the front seat. "We just walk out our door, put our boat in the water, and start paddling."

"I could definitely get used to this," Mom said.

We headed around the corner to Lake Union. We'd passed several other houseboat docks, but there was a certain houseboat Mom was determined we see.

I had a feeling she was taking me to see the houseboat from *Sleepless in Seattle*, a movie we'd watched about eleven times already. I'd also gone past the boat on a tour with Grandma earlier in the summer.

Mom pulled her paddle hard on the starboard side for the next two strokes so that we took a sharp turn to the left.

"Let's hug the shore on this side," she said. "As you can see, we're on the opposite side of the lake from the *Sleepless* house, in case you were worried I was going to make you go by it. There are some other things I want to show you." She'd recently read a book about floating homes in Seattle and was hot to show off her new knowledge. Mom was always reading all these random books and articles, which, she said, made her an expert on absolutely nothing but a darn good Trivial Pursuit and *Jeopardy!* player. Her arsenal of knowledge (or random facts) could sometimes be interesting, when it wasn't annoying. This time it was pretty interesting, as she pointed out a houseboat that actually had a basement with a fitness center and a wine cellar. As I struggled to wrap my head around the idea of a houseboat with a basement, we went by small, tidy floating homes that looked similar to the ones on our Portage Bay dock. We also went by some floating homes that were more like floating mansions, kind of like the huge beige houses you see out in the suburbs. Mom and her friend Mary Perez call them McMansions. It seemed odd and out of scale to see a McMansion next to a tiny wood cottage.

"I feel like we're a million miles away from our real life," I said to Mom. "Almost like we're in a different country or something."

"That, my dear daughter, is exactly where we're about to be."

"Does that mean you're going to make me keep

paddling until we get to Canada? Yikes! Hey, what's that?" I'd just spied a houseboat with colorful art and sculptures surrounding it. A flag with a white background flew at full mast from a large pole. The upper left corner of the flag had diagonal yellow and orange stripes; floating off center in the white area were some light blue stripes. The flag, the house, and the dock looked so colorful and chaotic compared to the tidy houses at the neighboring docks. I loved it immediately.

"That's the Archipelago of Tui Tui," Mom said excitedly.

"Huh?" My mind was combing back over the vocabulary lists and geography lessons from sixth grade. Archipelago, archipelago. Right! *Archipelago: A group of islands in a large body of water.*

But that didn't make any sense.

"Where's the island?" I asked.

"The house itself is an island nation," Mom said. "The owner seceded from the United States. He even has his own currency and postage stamps." As if on cue, when Mom said "owner," a man walked out on the dock and waved to us. At least I thought he was waving to us. I waved back, but then he seemed to be glaring at us, as if he'd just noticed us.

"You're making this all up, aren't you?" I asked.

"Good afternoon, neighbors!" I looked behind us and saw another kayak coming up quickly. It was Alice Campbell. "Small world, isn't it? I'm just on my way to Tui Tui. I'll be back in the United States soon enough." She pulled up alongside the island nation of Tui Tui and put a soft-side Polar Bear thermal bag on the dock. It was one of those coolers that holds only about a six-pack of soda. She was talking to the man on the dock, who was gesturing and pointing out in the water. Who was he? The king of Tui Tui? The prime minister? Or just Mr. Tui Tui? And how did a houseboat in the middle of Seattle become an independent state? I still couldn't believe this was true, and I intended to do some research as soon as I got back to my laptop.

Mr. Tui Tui held up a glass jar filled with liquid and showed it to Alice before putting it in the cooler. He put two more jars in the cooler, which she then stowed in her kayak's cargo area. He helped her push off from the dock and waved her on her way.

I watched as Alice paddled east toward Portage Bay. Mom steered us over to Aqua Verde Café, the restaurant that Jake had given us the gift certificate for. We could pull right up in our kayak, and the dockhand would help us out and pull our boat out—sort of like valet parking for kayaks. It's my absolute favorite restaurant in Seattle, and even though I've been kayaking since I was in kindergarten, it was the first time I'd pulled up in my own boat. Yeah, I know, it's not really my kayak. But I was feeling pretty richie-rich right about then.

CHAPTER 4

I WOKE UP the next morning to some obnoxious knocking. I waited for Mom to answer, but she must have been in the bathroom getting ready to go to work.

"Hello! Anyone in there?" A voice now accompanied the knocking. Mango answered the question with a series of barks.

"Oh great. Just my luck. No one's home but they left a dog in here. Joshua is going to go ballistic about this," a woman's voice muttered. She started rapping on the door again, a little more aggressively, as if her noise would make someone—other than a barking dog—appear.

Mom doesn't like me to answer the door when she's in the shower, but this knocking and barking had to stop. "Mango! Quiet! Good boy," I cooed. "Who's there on the other side of the door? Because there's about a dozen of us on this side."

"A dozen? Just my luck that there'd be twelve people in the way," the voice on the other side whined. "Wait. You're kidding, right?"

I didn't reply. Let her sweat it out, with me and my eleven friends on the Extreme Quiet Team. "Listen, I'm with the film crew, and we've got to make sure that everyone's out before we start filming today. Didn't they leave you a production schedule?"

"No, I don't have a production schedule," I said, trying to sound like an annoyed adult executive. "Let me check with my mom." That last comment kind of blew my cover.

I stuck my head into the bathroom and asked my mom if she had any idea what was going on.

"I completely forgot about the filming schedule," she said. "I'm so sorry. I shouldn't have said I'd work this morning. Let's see if Lily's family can come get you."

"I can take care of myself," I said. "I'm used to spending time alone."

"I know, I know. But this is different. You won't have anywhere to go."

I could see her point. I didn't much like the idea of Mango and me hanging out on a park bench all day.

I went back to the woman who was waiting at the door. "Can't I just stay inside if we don't make any noise? I won't be any trouble," I tried one last time, trying to stand tall and look older.

"Sorry, but no," said the young woman with the clipboard. "You don't look like the troublemaking type. It's just that Joshua, the continuity guy, will have a total freak-out if any little thing changes from scene to scene."

"Okay, I'll leave, but it's my opinion that an occasional background noise, such as a dog bark, could add a little authenticity to your show." I started pulling my sandals on and tossing keys, dog treats, poop bags, a water bottle, my camera, and my cell phone into my messenger bag.

"I agree completely. But my boss won't. I'm just the P.A.," she said.

I looked at her blankly.

"Production assistant. I'm just the production assistant. My name is Celeste, by the way. This is only my second P.A. gig. But I learned the hard way earlier this year that even if you think everything is the same, Joshua can spot the teensiest detail changing from shot to shot. You could open a window a crack, or change the blinds. And then I'll hear about it. Like that leaf." She was off whisking a leaf off the dock. I watched her with fascination, until something else caught my eye.

An older woman dressed in a black nylon tracksuit peered around the corner of the cottage next to ours. Mom had confirmed last night that no one was home next door to us. It might make sense that house cleaners were there yesterday, but why would someone be back so soon? Or so early in the day? Our eyes met briefly, and then she backed around the corner again. I was tempted to say, "Hey, Celeste, what about that woman? How come you aren't on her case to leave?" But someone else was demanding the production assistant's attention.

"Celeste! We're ready to set up. Everything ready on your end?"

"Just about," Celeste said. She turned toward me, adding, "I need this place cleared out in ten minutes, okay?" While Celeste's back was turned, the woman in black did a modified speedwalk down the dock and toward the street. She carried two large white buckets, one in each hand. They must have been empty, because those things were almost two feet tall and they didn't seem to slow her down.

I closed the door and gave Mom the update. In the few minutes that I had spent talking to Celeste, she had already managed to get in touch with Lily's dad—who was going to come pick up Mango and me—and was nearly ready to leave for work. Within five minutes, she and I were headed toward the street.

It was like a different world had sprung up while we slept. Large white umbrellas and light boxes were set up along the dock. Three huge white trucks and trailers, the kind without any logos or names, were taking up most of the street. A police officer was directing cars to turn off Boyer and onto side streets. Any doubts I'd had about whether they were really making a legitimate TV show here vanished. These trucks were the real thing. Seattle isn't exactly New York or L.A., but the city gets a surprising amount of movie, TV, and commercial action. I've spent enough time downtown to know that those seemingly nondescript cargo trucks and vans carry lights, metal rigging, cameras, and tons of other equipment. Even the food wagon is usually unmarked. It's like they're trying to go all incognito by not drawing attention to themselves, but the mere fact that a series of these vehicles are parked on a street is like a beacon proclaiming, "Hollywood has come to your little town." It makes me think of a movie star wearing dark sunglasses—inside.

"Hannah!"

"Wow, I can't believe you made it down here already" I said to Dan, Lily's dad.

"Well, as soon as Lily heard the words 'film' and 'crew,' there was no way she was going to miss out on the action," Dan said. "She practically pushed me out the door as soon as I got off the phone."

"Let's go see who's here," Lily said, smoothing some watermelon-flavored balm on her lips. We headed back to the dock, leaving my mom and Dan to figure out the game plan for the rest of the day.

"You're hoping to get picked up as an extra, aren't you?" I asked.

"Aren't *you*?" Lily, the aspiring actress, asked, cocking her right eyebrow. "Check this out! I finally perfected the one-eyebrow-up-at-a-time look! Anyway, we can make some money and get discovered. It will probably just be the first of many film roles for me, but at least you'll get a little spending money and the joy of seeing your name in credits this one time."

"Thanks for all the confidence you have in me," I said. Lily blew me a kiss and put on her sunglasses.

"Look out!" said a bearded guy balancing a six-foot metal contraption on top of his shoulder. He'd just missed a woman in black rain gear who had come off the dock, and then the beam swung toward us. Lily and I jumped to the side. The woman must have had a part in the movie, which would explain why she was wearing a waterproof get up—in black, no less—on a sunny Seattle day.

"So, who's in this movie anyway?" Lily asked.

"I have no idea," I said. "I don't even know what they're—"

"Aaaaarrrrgggghhhh!" A high-pitched scream interrupted me mid-sentence. Then a splash and . . .

Another scream. This time louder and shriller, coming from out by the dock where the film crew was.

Maybe it was part of the TV show, but it's true what they say about heart-stopping, bloodcurdling screams. My heart felt all panicky, and my blood felt weird. That's some good acting going on.

Only it turns out it wasn't acting.

"They're dead!" a woman screamed. "They're all dead!"

CHAPTER 5

MANGO YANKED HIS leash and started running toward the dock. I went along, as if I had any choice when a seventy-five-pound dog with the strength of a two-hundred-pound adult was pulling me. Then again, it's not as if I wasn't willing. Something big was happening.

"What if we get down there and find out it was part of the script?" Lily said, running alongside Mango and me.

I slowed down a tiny bit and pulled the pooch back, too. "That would be kind of embarrassing," I admitted.

"You can't just run toward danger, Hannah," Lily said. "We could ruin the shot."

That slowed me down even more. "Shot? We could get shot?"

"No! We could *ruin* the shot. As in, get in the way of the camera."

"That definitely could be kind of embarrassing," I said.

"It's not just kind of embarrassing. It's completely and unforgivingly embarrassing," Lily said.

A bout of embarrassment wasn't going to stop Mango

and me, however. I have a nose for crime, and I could smell something going on. Well, I couldn't actually *smell* anything going on, although some sort of aroma had definitely piqued Mango's interest. There was a lot of commotion and splashing at the end of the dock.

"Let's just check it out," I said to Lily.

"No one will notice us."

"I can't work in these conditions," a weepy and extremely wet woman said as two men helped pull her out of Lake Washington. Another woman immediately draped a blanket around the shivering actress. "The original script I approved didn't have a water shot," she said. Her teeth chattered, but her voice projected loud and clear. "I agreed to be a good sport today and go along with your changes, Marcus. But there are dead fish in the water! I think I touched them."

Dead fish? I looked over the edge of the dock where we stood, expecting to see some foot-long salmon belly up or something. But I couldn't see anything except dark water. I tightened my grip on Mango's leash.

"Who is that?" I whispered to Lily. I expect her to know the names of famous people since her mom gets *People* magazine, but Lily just shrugged. She was intently taking in the film scene.

The wet actress was chewing out a man with a baseball cap and black-framed sunglasses. "You're going to have to call a wrap for today, Marcus. I absolutely cannot work in these conditions. You'll need to rewrite this scene for me," she said, shrugging off a second blanket that some woman was trying to drape around her. "And I expect to have my shoes replaced by the time I get to the hotel." One of the crew members had just pulled a high-heeled green-and-gold sandal out of the water. He started to hand it to her, but she turned away from him. "Not that one! I want new shoes," she screeched. "Cynthia! Call the salon at Gene Juarez. Tell them it's an emergency and they need to get me in for a full Dead Sea salt scrub and wrap. I'll definitely need a hot stone massage as well."

"Yes, Miss Heathcliff," replied a young woman with a clipboard and a cell phone.

"Monica, please," the baseball cap man said. "It's just a little lake water. Think of it as getting back to nature."

"Marcus, I assure you, dead fish are not part of nature." The actress narrowed her eyes and scowled at the man she'd called Marcus. She tossed aside the blanket she'd been given and teetered toward the street in a left-right and up-down motion, since she had on only one high-heeled shoe.

"Monica," he called after her. "You're absolutely right to take the rest of the day off. Get some rest. We'll talk tonight."

"So that's Monica Heathcliff," Lily said to me. "I didn't recognize her soaking wet." The name didn't mean anything to me, and so far I wasn't too impressed with this actress's people skills.

"Okay, everyone, let's take a break. Be back here in forty-five. We'll need to get some more shots with this same lighting."

They were breaking after about fifteen minutes of working? Maybe I could get interested in this Hollywood scene.

"Hey, girls, what are you doing out here?" Mom rushed up behind us.

"That's exactly what I want to know," the guy named Marcus said, glaring at us. "What are you doing on my set?"

Mom immediately held out her hand and said, "I'm Maggie West, the house sitter for one of the residents on the dock."

"Marcus Dartmouth, director, *Dockside Blues,*" he said, in that fast-clipped way people who think they're important always introduce themselves on TV shows.

"Nice to meet you," Mom said. "The girls were just—"

But Marcus Dartmouth, director, interrupted her. "The house sitter? The sister, right? What a cushy gig. Excuse me!" He abruptly turned away and started barking out commands to a guy and a girl schlepping around lights and big white umbrellas.

"Whose sister are you?" Lily asked.

"I have absolutely no idea who or what he's talking about," Mom said. She didn't exactly answer Lily, but that's because Lily knows everyone in our family and was well aware of the fact that Mom was an only child. Just like me.

"Maybe he thinks you look like Monica Heathcliff when she's dry," I said.

"I'm sure he thinks that my frizzed-out curly hair and the dark circles under my eyes make me look just like a movie star," Mom said sarcastically.

"Excuse me, but you need to clear the dock." It was Celeste, the P.A.

"Right, we were just—" Mom started to say.

"Now, actually. You need to clear it now."

What's with these Hollywoodesque folks? They never seem to let Mom finish a sentence. Celeste was full of bravado, but she looked more nervous than before. A short man in a fedora stood about twenty feet down the dock watching her. He flipped open a cell phone and punched in a couple of numbers. Celeste's phone rang, and she answered immediately.

"Get rid of them," the man down the dock said into the phone. This must be the notorious Joshua.

Hello! Standing close enough to hear you, mister. I couldn't help but stare at him.

"Right away," Celeste said. They flipped their phones shut at the same time.

"Sorry, we're just leaving," I said, hoping her boss would be impressed with her for getting us set-crashers out of the way.

"Let's go," Mom said. She sounded impatient, with a tone that doesn't often creep into her voice.

Mom and Lily were already halfway toward the street, but I was purposely lagging behind. Mango wasn't that excited to leave familiar territory, which turned out to be helpful cover for me as I watched the woman in the black tracksuit—the one whom I had spotted while I was talking to Celeste. She was crouching low on the dock, scooping water by the spot where Monica Heathcliff had fallen into the water. I was pretty sure it wasn't the same woman I had seen in the black rain gear.

Maybe this was part of the TV crew, too, but she didn't seem like the Hollywood type. Then again, maybe she had some sort of behind-the-scenes job. From what I could tell so far, there was one actress and about thirty other people working hard to make her look good. Maybe this woman was part of the continuity team and her job was to make sure that every molecule of water looked the same from scene to scene.

Mango barked a short, friendly yip, and the woman turned.

It was Alice.

I knew she saw us, but she didn't wave. Or even smile. She turned back to the water.

"What's the scoop?" Lily asked.

"Scoop? Speaking of scooping, look over there," I said. But by the time I turned to where Alice had been scooping water, she was gone. "Never mind," I muttered. "Let's get away from these people."

"I want you to stay at Lily's house for the day," Mom said as Lily climbed into the Shannons' car. She was climbing into our beat-up Honda to drive to her shift at Wired. "I get off work at around three, and I'll come pick you up there."

"You don't have to do that," I said, feeling guilty about making Mom go out of her way. "I can just take the number 66 back from Maple Leaf."

"But you'll have Mango with you," she pointed out. "He can ride Metro. He just needs a ticket," I said. I guess Mom never realized that dogs could ride the bus. Working dogs—like guide dogs and service dogs—can ride for free, which makes total sense. Lapdogs can also ride for free. Big dogs, like Mango, pay full fare, which means he ends up paying more than I do for a "youth" ticket.

"That's good to know," Mom said. "But I'll still plan to come get you. Mango might not be as comfortable on public transportation as you are."

Dan drove the nearly four miles through city neighborhoods and the University of Washington area up to Maple Leaf, the neighborhood where Mom and I used to live before she was laid off from MegaComp. Those seemed like the good old days: We lived in a two-bedroom house with a nice yard and an alley that was perfect for skateboarding. Our house was just three blocks away from where Lily, my best friend since second grade at Olympic View Elementary, lives.

It's pretty fun to get to live in different parts of Seattle, especially when we get to live in rich people's neighborhoods, like a couple months ago when we lived downtown at the Belltown Towers. I doubted there were many soon-to-be-seventh graders in Seattle who lived on houseboats, too. Still, I'd give anything to be back in our old neighborhood with my friends nearby.

Chapter 6

THE WHITE CARGO vans were pulling out just as we returned to Portage Bay that afternoon. Mom pulled our Honda easily into a prime space close to the dock.

Mom, Mango, and I got out of our car and started walking slowly toward the dock.

A silver two-door hatchback with red tape over a taillight and music blaring out of the open windows came to a screeching halt on the street. The driver put the car into reverse and zipped into another prime parking space right in front of ours. The car's right rear wheel bumped up on the curb and onto the grass. The car pulled forward and thudded into the spot, then shuddered to a stop. It seemed so quiet as soon as the car stereo turned off.

I might be a few years away from my driver's license, but even I could tell that there was no reason to have to go over the curb.

The door creaked open and a woman with jet black hair in a high ponytail climbed out of the driver's seat. She was wearing yoga pants, a short tank top, and flip-flops.

She saw us and gave a half smile, and then headed up the sidewalk to our dock.

"Do you live here?" Mom asked, all hyper-friendly, probably to make up for the judgmental thoughts she was trying to crowd out of her head. The ponytailed woman scowled at her.

"I don't mean to pry or anything," Mom said, talking superfast now. "It's just that we're house-sitting for one of the residents on this dock, and we haven't met the neighbors yet."

The woman kept walking toward the dock. "I'm just a house sitter, too," she said, not even looking at us.

I noticed the way she said "just" before "house sitter." Should I just resent her for making it sound as if Mom and I were low-lifes for living for free in someone else's home?

"Oh, what luck to catch you all at the same time!" Alice Campbell met us as we walked up the dock. "Maggie and Hannah, this is Estie Bartlett. She's taking care of Luci Mack's house and two cats for a couple of weeks."

Estie gave us another half smile. Wow. Add it to the earlier one she gave us, and you'd have a whole smile. A forced smile, but a whole one.

"It's a rare occasion when we have two house sitters on our dock," Alice said. "That calls for a party. Or at least an informal gathering so you can meet all your neighbors."

"That sounds lovely," Mom said.

"I know you must be anxious to get back to your homes.

I'm so sorry that the blasted film crew displaces us all during the day," Alice continued. She was a fast talker, but in a happy enthusiastic way.

"Didn't they allow anyone to stay at all?" I asked Alice. I tried to say it casually, but I wanted her to know I'd seen her on the film set.

"They insisted that everyone leave. That production assistant, Celeste, had me out of my own house first thing this morning. I spent most of the day at the downtown library. It was my day to volunteer as a tour guide. If you haven't toured the library, you simply must," Alice went on.

I noticed she hadn't directly answered my question. Yes, the crew of *Dockside Blues* had insisted that everyone leave. She also spent "most of the day" away. Was she just talking, or was she purposefully avoiding saying that she had been at the edge of the dock where the dead fish were?

"How did *Dockside Blues* end up on this particular dock?" Mom asked.

"Oh, the director has a connection. He grew up in Seattle, you know," Alice said. "Anyway, I hope you have some time to come over and join us on my deck this evening. The neighbors who are here are all anxious to meet you. Let's say six o'clock?"

"Great," Mom said. "What can we bring?"

"Oh, please. Just bring yourselves. We want to welcome you to the community," Alice said.

"I'll see if I'm feeling well enough to make it," the other

house sitter said. She walked toward the first cottage on the left, unlocked the door, and quickly entered and closed the door behind her.

"I'll see you at six, then," Alice said. "Hannah, this could be a good opportunity for you to hand out your business cards to the other residents in the Floating Home Association. I'm sure some of your neighbors could use your help with errands or could recommend you as a dog walker for their friends. In any event, I'll see you in a few hours."

Mom and I continued on to our new home. Finally! Mango was practically jumping up and down, he was so excited to get back inside. Mom fumbled with the keys until she unlocked the shiny purple door. She held the door open for me. Mango took off, immediately going inside to reclaim his territory and chase his cat. I was still hyperaware of the motion of being on the water. It felt weird—being in the safety of a house while it moves. Still, I was pretty sure I could get used to this walking-on-water business.

CHAPTER 7

"HANNAH? HANNAH? Wake up, dear," a voice from far, far away seemed to be calling to me.

I tried to push it out of my dreams, but it came back. "Hannah?"

I woke up with a start. Not only was I in a strange bed sleeping with a huge beast, but a total stranger was nudging me awake.

"I'm awake!" I said as convincingly as I could.

I pushed myself up on one elbow and looked around to get my bearings. Okay. I was in the bedroom/office in Jake Heard's houseboat. The beast next to me was a drooling labradoodle named Mango. I glanced at my disco clock radio that I'd set next to the bed and saw that it was 6:30 at night. And Alice Campbell was waking me from a pretty darn good dream that I'm pretty sure included tin roof sundaes on a gently rocking boat.

"I didn't mean to startle you, but I wanted to make sure you and Mango make it to the dockside party," she said.

"Right," I said slowly.

"I've been meaning to tell you something," Alice said. That got my attention. I sat up immediately. Mango got up, too, and went into that downward dog yoga pose that is possibly one of the most aptly named maneuvers in the world.

"I wanted to tell you my whole name," Alice continued. "It's Alice Kawamoto Campbell."

She must have seen the "ah-ha" moment in my eyes. "You were wondering, weren't you?" she asked.

I nodded. "I thought maybe you were Japanese, but I wasn't sure, and then I was kind of embarrassed that I even wondered."

"You should never be embarrassed to ask what you want to know. I would have understood if you'd asked me if I were Japanese. Or whatever. Just like I'd like to ask you if you're Chinese."

"Yep. Born in China. Adopted by Maggie and moved to Seattle. Was Kawamoto your maiden name?" I asked.

"It was, and it is. It is still my family name. Now I use it as my middle name. I keep it safe between my first and last names."

I liked that. I was liking Alice Kawamoto Campbell.

Then I remembered that she was sneaking around the set of *Dockside Blues* and at the island nation of Tui Tui. She was up to something, and I wanted to know what. Would it be rude to ask? Or worse, would I be asking something I really didn't want to know the answer to? I wasn't so sure I wanted to know if this nice woman was involved in something shady.

"Hannah, please remember that if you want to know something, you need only to ask. I'll tell you what I can," she said.

Did she really mean it? I wasn't so sure. "Did you say party?" I asked, standing.

Alice smiled at me. "We're just firing up the barbecue. Follow me."

The Portage Bay dock party would have been a total bore if it wasn't on the water. Maybe rich people in general are total bores, but we don't always notice right away because the packaging and surroundings are interesting. Nah. I had to swallow that ugly, jealous thought. I have a tendency to resent people with money for the simple fact that they have money. And we don't.

There might even be interesting people right there, but all the adults were talking about the Floating Home Association and committees and something-or-other about action with so-and-so on the city council. I tuned it all out and sat in a comfy high-back wood deck chair with a lemonade slushy and my camera. I had a fresh roll of 36-exposure black-and-white film, and I'd promised Lily I'd get photos of any celebrities who might stop by. Just in case.

"Estie! I'm delighted you could join us!" Alice said. She

handed a glass of iced tea to the other house sitter. With my well-developed and always subtle eavesdropping skills, I learned that Estie had been living there for about a week. She was taking care of two cats and she was a yoga teacher at one of those sweaty yoga places, where they keep the room superwarm.

"Who invited him?" Frank, the owner of the red cottage, asked, scowling at the sunglasses-clad man striding toward the dock.

"Oh, I did, Frank! We need more excitement around here," said Louisa, the woman from the blue cottage.

"Of course we do," Alice murmured.

Estie smoothed her tight pink T-shirt and tucked it in. She used her free hand to fluff her hair.

"Welcome, Marcus!" Louisa did that Hollywood kiss-kiss thing with Marcus Dartmouth, director, *Dockside Blues*.

"Aunt Alice! Always a pleasure to see you," Marcus said, giving Alice a stiff hug and pat on the back.

Did he say *aunt*? I stared at Alice.

"Marcus, I think you know most of my neighbors here," Alice said, "But let me introduce you to Estie Bartlett. She's house-sitting for Luci Mack."

"Yes, we met earlier today," Marcus said, extending his hand toward Mom. Estie looked crestfallen.

"I'm actually Maggie West. My daughter and I are house-sitting for Jake Heard at the end of the dock," Mom said. I could tell she was amused.

"Maggie, this is my nephew, Marc. Excuse me, *Marcus*. And Marcus, this is Maggie, and *this* is Estie," Alice said.

Marcus recovered his goof quickly, but he looked rather confused. Estie was practically glowing as she enthusiastically pumped Marcus's hand.

"I'm such a fan of your work, Mr. Dartmouth," she said. She said it like *Dart-mouth,* not *Dart-muth*, which is the way Marcus Dartmouth, director, *Dockside Blues*, says it.

"Please, call me"—I waited for him to say something like "Call me Marcus," but instead he finished—"Mr. *Dart-muth*." He pronounced it for her. He handed her his card and—I swear I saw this—winked at her. Estie, who was already showing a deep blush of embarrassment under her golden tan, turned even redder.

"Aunt Alice, have you seen Mum and Timothy lately?" Marcus asked. I swear I heard it just like that—he actually said "mum."

"No, dear, but I imagine you could probably catch them at the Emerald City Yacht Club on an evening like this," she said. "If they're not on the water, they're probably working on the *Clean Sweep*."

"Yes, I suppose I could drive down there and see," he said. "Although they might put me to work cleaning the bottom of that boat."

"Drive? It's just four blocks away! You've spent too much time in L.A. if you think you can't walk down the street," Frank's voice boomed. "Heck, you could jump in right here and swim down there. Might do you some good. Help you cool off and all that."

"I don't think I'd want to swim in that water right now," Louisa said.

"Frank! Please don't encourage anyone to go swimming in this water!" Alice said sternly.

"Were there really dead fish in the water today?" I asked.

Marcus took off his sunglasses and looked at me. His expression seemed to say, Who are you and why are you talking to me?

"I heard that actress, Monica, say she touched dead fish," I added.

"Monica has a tendency to overact sometimes. She is, after all, an actress," Marcus said.

"Yes, she is quite the actress," Estie said. "Always has been."

"There's nothing wrong with the water. The water is perfectly safe." Marcus stated it as if he was at a press conference on the TV news.

"She sounded pretty convincing," I said. "I mean, she really screams well."

Marcus tried to laugh. Only thing was, I wasn't trying to be funny.

CHAPTER 8

"LILY! ANSWER IF you're there." I waited for a few seconds. "Okay. Listen. The TV crew is going to be here again tomorrow at nine. See if you can get a ride down here before they start setting up. I have a plan."

I closed my cell phone and plugged it into the charger. Mom was on the deck, reading and watching the boats go by. I picked up my camera and headed out to join her. I had taken only a couple of photos at the dockside barbecue, and they were pretty uninspired. I was itching to experiment with the fading evening light and the long shadows that reached out into the lake water.

"Isn't this incredible?" Mom asked, putting her book down on the table. "If I block out the traffic noise from the bridge, I feel as if we're on a raft in the middle of the water. And all the boaters are so friendly." Mom waved to a motorboat and five shirtless teenage boys waved back.

"Did you have to wave to them?" I asked, mortified.

"I believe the friendly wave is part of the boating culture," she said. "I think they wave so they have an excuse for staring at the people on their decks and houseboats."

I fiddled with the camera's telephoto lens and looked through the viewfinder. I took a quick glance at the boys in the boat, but then kept the lens moving so Mom wouldn't think I was checking out boys.

"I wonder why so many boats are coming by right now," I said.

"We're close to the Emerald City Yacht Club, just a few blocks away. My guess is that people spent the day out in Lake Union or in the Puget Sound and they're heading back now that the sun is setting," Mom said.

"Is that the same yacht club that Marcus Dartmouth, director, mentioned?"

Mom granted me a laugh for the way I tried to say "Marcus Dartmouth, director" like I was a Hollywood hotshot. "Yes, it is. Alice told me that Marcus grew up on the other side of the arboretum, in a gated neighborhood called Broadmoor. Apparently his mother and stepfather have been big boaters since he was a young boy. Perhaps I should say they're 'yachters.'"

"What makes a boat a yacht?" I asked. "'Yacht' sounds so uppity."

"Attitude," Mom said.

"Huh?"

"Attitude is what makes a boat a yacht, although yacht owners might say that a boat has to be a certain length to be deemed a true yacht." Mom reached for her laptop, and

I picked up my camera and focused on a sailboat coming past us. I might be an obsessive artist, but my mom is beyond obsessive when it comes to checking things online. I knew I was about to be in for a definition of "yacht."

"Interesting," she said. "There doesn't seem to be one singular definition for 'yacht.' One dictionary says a yacht is a 'large usually motor-driven craft used for pleasure cruising.' It doesn't give a specific size. But some people claim that a vessel must be longer than thirty feet to be a yacht. Still others insist that it must be longer than sixty-five feet, or somewhere between sixty-five and one hundred fifty feet."

"Yowza. Those are some big boats they're talking about," I said.

"You mean *yachts*. It goes back to my original observation: It's all about attitude."

Now I had a front-row seat to watch this boating, sailing, and yachting crowd. I picked up the camera again, moving the lens from boat to boat. There wasn't any wind, so even the sailboats had to use motors to putter through the bay. I clicked a photo of a large motorboat—probably long enough to qualify as a yacht—with wood trim. The name *Clean Sweep* was painted in an ornate style on the side. A man in a captain's hat sat in the driver's seat, puttering along. He killed the engine and let the boat rock gently in the wake of the other boats. An older woman with bright blond hair peered at the exterior side of the boat. I took another picture just as she grimaced. The man shook his head and lifted a large plastic bucket and sat it on the bench seat in the back. The woman used a smaller plastic bucket to scoop something out. She leaned far over the side of the boat and dropped something in the water. The man nudged her and pointed over to us. I quickly lowered the camera and gave a big, friendly boating wave.

They didn't wave back.

CHAPTER 9

THE NEXT MORNING I awoke to a wet nose and the sound of tap-dancing toenails. Mango needed to go to the bathroom.

"You're such a polite dog," I told him as I hooked his retractable leash to his collar. Instead of barking for attention, Mango seemed to like to do a little potty dance on the wood floor of the houseboat. It must be the Standard poodle in him.

Mom had already left to work the breakfast shift at Wired Café downtown. As I walked out of our houseboat, two newspapers, the *New York Times* and the *Seattle Times*, were waiting on our welcome mat. Pretty spiffy aim if the paper carrier could land the newspapers right on our doorstep without veering off into the water. I took the blue plastic wrapper from the *New York Times* just in case I needed a poop bag. Mango was high-stepping down the wood dock, obviously anxious to get to the small grassy patch by the mailboxes. "We're almost there, fella," I said to the dog.

"Good morning!" the neighbor who I think was named

Frank called out to us. "Mango taking you out to stretch your legs?" He was watering the flowers in the dozen or more planters arranged on his deck.

I nodded and held up the blue plastic bag from the newspaper.

Frank laughed. "Glad to see you got your paper and that you have multiple uses for it. The papers come to the mailboxes around five in the morning. I bring them all up after my six o'clock run."

"Wow. That's nice. Thanks."

"No problem."

Mango and I walked along Boyer Avenue. We stopped at the Canal Market because one of us was enticed by a pink-frosted doughnut from the extra-yummy Top Pot bakery. The other one of us waited outside patiently for a doggie treat. We turned around and passed our dock, continuing down several blocks until I came to the forbidding entrance to the Emerald City Yacht Club.

"Oh, excuse me!" I said, jumping back as the locked gate swung open and almost slammed into my face.

"Yes," said the woman who came out from the private yacht club. Was she saying, "Yes, excuse you"? That wasn't very polite. I'd try to make up for her lack of small-talk skills with some extra polite talk of my own.

"Gorgeous morning for boating. Are you just going out?"

"No," she said. She was holding the gate open and glancing behind her.

"Come on, Timothy," she said.

"Coming, Stella," came a voice, along with a man in a captain's hat whom I recognized from last night.

"I believe I saw you in your boat last night," I said.

"It's a yacht," the woman said.

"Right. I think I saw you in your yacht right before sunset. It's gorgeous."

"If you think these compliments will get you a ride on the *Clean Sweep*, you'll have to come back another day." The man smiled affably at me. "I just docked her after our morning, er, our morning . . ."

Now he seemed to be stumbling for words.

"Our morning errand," the woman finished for him. "Give me the bag." He handed her an open-top canvas tote bag. As she quickly rummaged through it, I saw a glimpse of what looked like a black Gore-tex rain jacket and rain pants. I tried to picture her wearing them.

"Took a while to get her cleaned up," Timothy was saying. "The plants are pretty thick in the lake right now. They wreak havoc on the hull. But we got her all tidy, and she's as gorgeous as ever now," the man said. I assumed he was still talking about his boat. Or yacht. Whatever. He was pretty nice, but my attention was focused on her. This was the third time I'd seen this same woman. I was sure she'd been on our dock when we first moved in and yesterday morning when the TV crew was setting up.

"Well, good-bye then," I said, attempting another

friendly boating wave as they walked off.

Once again, I didn't get a wave back. So much for the friendly, waving boating crowd. Make that *yachting* crowd.

As Mango and I were returning from our walk, I spotted Lily and her dad.

"Hannah!" Lily hopped off the hood of her dad's car and came rushing over to us. "My parents said I can stay here with you all day."

"Lily, call us before dinner," her dad called. "Stay dry, girls."

"I thought your dad would want to see our houseboat," I said as Dan Shannon drove off.

"He's dying to see it. But he's on his way to meet a bunch of people for some big bike ride for the Cascade Bicycle Club," she said. "So what's the plan? I hope it's about how to get onto *Dockside Blues*. You have to tell me everything Marcus Dartmouth said last night. Whoa! Who's that doing those power yoga moves?"

"Doing what?" I followed Lily's finger, which was pointing to the first cottage on the left. Inside, Estie was doing some kind of handstand maneuver. Her body was in an upside-down crouching position with all her weight balanced on her hands. She stayed motionless.

"That's the heron position. Or crane. Or some kind of bird," Lily whispered. "I saw it in a yoga book. Who's the yogini?"

"She's another house sitter," I said. As I said it, the word "sister" almost came spilling out. House sitter. Sister. "Maybe she's the sister house sitter that director dude was talking about," I said.

"Which would make her Monica Heathcliff's sister! Which would make her a good person for us to get to know if we want to get a role on *Dockside Blues*."

"I dunno. Her name is Estie Bartlett, not Estie Heathcliff," I said.

"Oh, come on! Heathcliff is so obviously a made-up name. It's so obvious it's almost embarrassing for the person who thought it up," Lily said, smiling.

"And Estie's hair is black, but Monica's is blond."

"And I'd bet that neither color is natural," Lily said.

"Good morning!" Alice Campbell was just getting out of her bright red kayak. She pulled a black soft-side cooler out from the cargo area. I stooped down to help her lift the kayak out of the water.

"Thank you! It's so much easier with two people." She dried her hands on her pants and held one out to Lily. "Nice to see you again, Lily."

"It's tough, but as Hannah's best friend, I'm obligated to stand by her during this incredibly difficult time while she's living on a houseboat," Lily said.

Alice laughed. "I'm afraid we'll have another day of film crew disruptions in our midst today. Marcus assures me there will be only a few days on location here. They'll do the rest back at the studio in Los Angeles."

I saw Lily's eyebrows go up with interest as Alice referred to the director, Marcus, so casually.

"Is Marcus really your nephew?" I blurted out.

"He is, indeed. You seem surprised."

"He just doesn't seem like he'd be related to you. He's not as nice. No offense to your nephew or anything," I added hurriedly.

Luckily, Alice laughed. "I thought you were going to say we don't look alike," she said. "Marcus is good underneath that Hollywood act of his. He's always been special to me. His father was my husband's brother. Unfortunately, both of the Campbell brothers died in a car accident many years ago. Marcus's mother, Stella, immediately remarried. Marcus was adopted by his stepfather, Timothy Dartmouth."

Okay. I'm not dense. I'd already figured that the man and woman I'd seen seen at the yacht club were Marcus's parents. Or at least I assumed they were. How many couples named Stella and Timothy could there be who have a boat—er, excuse me, a *yacht*—called the *Clean Sweep*?

"His parents really like to keep their boat shipshape, don't they? They were already cleaning it this morning," I said.

Alice gave me a sharp glance. Her tone of voice was markedly different as she said, "You saw the *Clean Sweep*? When? Where was it? Do you remember what time?"

Whoa on the barrage of questions. "Um, I saw it last night when it was getting dark. It was out there," I pointed. "I think they were out this morning, too. Mango and I just ran into them when they were leaving Emerald City Yacht Club."

"So they were already out this morning, were they? I was out on the water by seven, but I didn't see them. I'll have to get up earlier next time. What time do you think it was when they returned?"

I told her I'd seen them on the land, so I didn't really know. I wasn't at all sure why it was important. "Good, good. This is all good information, Hannah," Alice said distractedly. "Quite useful information." She grabbed the soft-side cooler and I heard glass jars clanking against one another inside. She was mumbling to herself, something about levels and minutes and evaporation. Alice looked me in the eyes. "Hannah, please tell me if you see the *Clean Sweep* again."

And with that, she quickly went into her houseboat and shut the door, leaving me with all sorts of questions spinning through my head. Why would Alice want to know if I saw Marcus Dartmouth's parents? Was she trying to hide something from them? Or were they hiding something from her? I suspected that Stella and Timothy were dumping something in the water. I've heard about lakes and ponds that are "stocked" with fish. People actually put fish into the water so that fishermen have better chances of catching something. Was it possible that Marcus's parents were trying to stock this part of the lake? Maybe they'd chosen the wrong kind of fish or something.

Oh, ick. Maybe they were dumping dead fish in the lake. Nah, that's crazy.

CHAPTER 10

I'M NOT QUITE following all this," Lily said, as Mango led us down the L-shaped dock to our cottage. I filled her in as best I could.

"If these people have a yacht four blocks away and she wants to see them, why doesn't she just go down there? Why does she have you on the lookout for this boat?" Lily asked.

"Plus, they're related. That makes it even weirder," I added.

Lily had me fill her in on every single word Marcus Dartmouth, director, had said the night before. None of it was terribly interesting, yet she hung onto every word.

"Did anyone last night say anything about needing extras? Because, you know, I'm here and ready to work," Lily said.

"I don't know. I had a feeling that the other house sitter is hoping for a role, too. I'm thinking that if they want this show to be a success, they'd cast Mango," I said, rewarding the dog with a belly rub since he was looking especially cute. "Maybe there's a part for him."

"Do you think that other house sitter has a chance at a role?" she asked.

"I have no idea."

"I wonder if they'd put Mango's name in the credits," Lily mused. "Maybe I should change my name. You know, have a better stage name. Lily Newman. Lily Pacino. Lily Lang, Lily . . ."

A rap on the wood frame of the cottage door interrupted Lily and sent Mango into a series of barks.

"Hello? I need to ask for your cooperation this morning," a high-pitched voice called from the doorway. I hadn't even said "come in" or anything when Celeste, the production assistant, walked inside. "Yes, yes, Joshua. I have it all under control. I'll use the Polaroids." I looked behind her to see where Joshua was, and then I realized she was having two conversations at once: one with us and the other on the headset of her cell phone.

"Now, girls, here are the Polaroids of the set from yesterday. I need to close the blinds to the exact same degree as in this shot." She handed a photograph to me. "See what you can do to match this photo. Then you're free to leave."

Lily and I stared at her. She sighed. "Please. *Please* see if you can match this photo," she said. "I'm sorry if I sound snappish, but Joshua is such a demanding continuity guy. We have to finish the shots we didn't get yesterday because, because . . . because Miss Heathcliff needed to leave early."

"Yeah, I heard she had a spa emergency. Ow!" Lily kicked me along the side of my leg, nailing my ankle-bone. "Watch it," I muttered to her.

"You watch it," she whispered.

Celeste was fighting back a smile. She regained her stony-faced production assistant look and got all businesslike again. "Monica was a little concerned because she thought she touched something dead in the water," Celeste said. "You know how sometimes seaweed or leaves touch your toes in the water and it spooks you. That's all it was. Anyway, girls, if you could help me out, it would be great. Oh, and don't forget that you need to be out of here before we start filming."

She pivoted around on spikey heeled flip-flops. Two steps down the dock and one of the heels went down between two wood planks, sending her sprawling. Like we didn't see that one coming.

I rushed over to her and helped her up. "Are you okay?"

"I'm okay. Embarrassed, but okay." She took off her flip-flops and hurled them into the water, immediately bursting into a fit of giggles. Lily and I exchanged looks. I'm pretty independent, but I am in no position to deal with some random adult's mental illness or emotional breakdown.

"Um, do you want us to try to get your shoes out of the water?" I asked. Mango crouched in his classic downward dog yoga pose at the edge of the dock, wagging his tail and eyeing one of Celeste's sandals as if it were a tennis ball waiting for retrieval.

"No, thanks. They were stupid shoes anyway. I bought them last night just to try to look more, more...I don't know what more I was looking for actually," she said, getting up to her feet and dusting off her white pants. "Maybe I was hoping uncomfortable shoes would make me act tougher or something."

"Uncomfortable shoes just make me whine," I said. Lily had grabbed a kayak paddle and was trying to move the shoes closer to her.

"You can have them if you get them," Celeste told her. "I've got some sneakers in my car. I'll be more human in my own shoes."

Celeste's bare feet padded gingerly along the wood dock back to the street.

"Fetch, Mango!" Lily instructed the Labrador retriever and poodle mix. Instantly the dog made a splash into the water and headed for one of the sandals.

"Lily! Why did you do that? Now Celeste will get in trouble because the dock is wet and that Joshua guy will yell at her and maybe even fire her," I said.

"It's a dock! Docks get wet." She accepted one of the sandals from Mango's mouth and told him to fetch the other one. He happily turned around and continued his mission.

"We're going to have to wash the dog again," I whined.

"Oops, hadn't thought of that," Lily admitted. "But didn't Celeste just say that there was nothing to worry about?" She leaned over the edge of the dock again.

"Well, unlike you, I don't want to take any chances," I told her.

"Eureka!" Lily cried triumphantly, holding up both sandals. "Oh, and look! They fit!"

"Oh, and look . . . they look ridiculous," I added.

Mango made a move like he was about to shake, and I immediately backed up. No offense to the dog, but I didn't want any suspicious water drops on me, either. Alice had been so adamant about washing lake water off of him. If it was bad for the pooch, I bet it was bad for humans, too. "We need to get this dog washed," I said to Lily. She was still eyeing her feet and the sandals admiringly.

"The problem is, you have no eye for fashion," Lily said.

"I think we have a bigger problem right now," I said.

"Celeste was so nice to give these to me," Lily said.

"She is actually pretty nice," I said. "That's why I feel bad for what we're about to do."

CHAPTER 11

"WHAT? WE'RE GOING to do nothing? That seems so boring. Especially coming from you," Lily said. I'd filled her in on my plan while we washed Mango off in the shower. Now Lily was pivoting in half circles, admiring her new high-heeled sandals in front of the closet mirror upstairs in Jake's bedroom loft.

"Nothing. Absolutely nothing. You see, if we stay inside here, we can watch all the action firsthand. I thought you'd like that."

"I don't want to *watch* the action. I want to be on TV," Lily said.

"Really?" I used my best fake-astonishment voice. "Actually, Lily, nothing is brilliant." I had to pause and think through what I'd said. I'm not often making philosophical proclamations like that. "What I mean is, doing nothing is brilliant. The more we know about the script, the characters, and how things work, the easier it will be for us to get Marcus Dartmouth, director, to put us on the show."

"Us? You want to be on *Dockside Blues*, too?"

"You bet. I think they need some diversity on that show, based on all the white people we saw on the dock yesterday. Shhh! Someone's coming. Darn. I guess we're stuck here now."

"Darn," Lily said, smiling.

We crawled silently to the window, peering between two slats in the white blinds on the loft window. Two black-hooded shapes moved quickly along the dock, glancing behind them several times.

"Hold on," I whispered to Lily. I tiptoed down to my bedroom and grabbed my camera and an extra lens. Back upstairs, I put on the telephoto lens and wedged the long lens through the slats of the blinds and adjusted the focus until I could see the two faces crystal clear. Despite their melodramatic entrance and head movements, I knew they couldn't be part of the TV show. Unless Marcus Dartmouth had decided to give his mother and stepfather a couple of stealthy roles and they were rehearsing before the film crew arrived.

"What are they pouring out?" Lily whispered.

I took a couple of photographs. "It's not dead fish. Not even nondead fish," I said, backing away from the window, suddenly feeling overwhelmingly sad. "I'm afraid it might be something to kill fish, though. Something toxic."

We had just witnessed Timothy and Stella Dartmouth walking along the outer edge of the dock, each shaking a plastic bucket so that a white powder spewed into the water. It looked like laundry detergent, but I had a feeling it wasn't quite that simple. I hadn't seen what they'd emptied into the lake from their boat the other night, but I bet it was the same substance. I couldn't imagine what it was, but if we could figure that out, maybe we could figure out why the Dartmouths were pouring it into Lake Washington.

"We need to get a sample of the water as soon as possible," I said.

"And then what, Captain Science? Do we run some of our genius scientific experiments in our basement laboratory? Oops. We forgot to make a secret laboratory in the basement. Double oops! The basement of this houseboat would be underwater and kind of wet."

"Shhh!" I said as I watched Stella and Timothy skulk away in their matching black, hooded rain gear. Someone should tell them that villains use black *at night* because it helps them blend in. Head-to-toe black clothing on a sunny Seattle day was hardly going with the flow in terms of wardrobe choice.

Before I could even leave the loft window perch, another person came on the dock. Still not someone from *Dockside Blues*.

"What's she doing out here?" Lily whispered.

Estie, the other houseboat house sitter, peered around the corner of the Morrisons' cottage and then stepped out to the far side of the dock. She set down a fishing tackle box and swiftly plopped herself into a cross-legged sitting position. Then, just as quickly, she unfurled her legs, snapped the tackle box closed, and took refuge behind the gate at the Morrisons' cottage.

Alice Campbell came out on the dock, doing the same quiet walk and furtive glancing over her shoulder as the previous dockside visitors. She opened a thermal cooler bag and took out two jars. She took another look behind her and then began pouring something from one jar to the other. Then she dumped the mixture into the lake water. She took another jar out of the cooler and used it to scoop up some water. Then she took a fourth jar out of the cooler, unscrewed the top, and poured from this jar into the third jar. Alice closed all the jars, placed them carefully back in the black bag, and zipped the cooler shut.

As soon as Alice left, Estie was back on the dock with her tackle box. Why in the world were all these people so interested in the water here? Were they messing it up or cleaning it up? And why all the scurrying?

At that point, the setup crew arrived, and I suddenly understood why everyone was rushing around.

"We shouldn't have gone through the drive-thru at Starbucks," a man said as he and another man rolled a cart of equipment onto the dock. "It always takes longer to go through the drive-thru than to go inside and wait in the line. It's also a waste of gas."

As they approached, Estie hurriedly put her jars and

bottles back in the tackle box.

"No, no," the second man said. "It wastes more gas to turn off the engine and restart it."

"That's ridiculous. There's no way it could use more gas to go inside—"

A clatter of glass interrupted their debate when they came upon Estie, who was holding the open tackle box by the handle, while the contents rolled along the dock.

"Good thing nothing broke," one of the men said. "Joshua and Marcus wouldn't take too kindly to the dock being wet where it wasn't wet yesterday."

I grimaced, noticing that Mango's wet splashes were still visible on the dock.

"Sorry!" Estie said, grabbing bottles and scooping them back in her box.

"No harm done," the taller guy said. "But everyone should be off the dock before Marcus gets here."

Estie smoothed down her hair with her right hand. "Are you expecting Marcus soon?"

"Any minute. For some reason he wants to be here during setup today."

"I'll get out of your way then," Estie said.

"You look familiar," the other guy said. "Were you ever on *Love Today*? Not that I ever watched the daytime dramas."

"Ha! Anyone who says 'daytime drama' instead of 'soap opera' is definitely someone who watches them," the first man said.

The second guy shoved him a bit. "Nah. I didn't watch them. I could have worked on them though, you know. Been on the crew or something." They kept bickering as they started opening crates and unzipping black bags that protected equipment. Estie smiled and tossed her long dark hair over her right shoulder and walked back to her cottage, swishing her hips and holding the tackle box like it was a patent leather handbag.

"Exit stage left," Lily said as we watched Estie almost prance down the dock as if she were a model on a runway.

Watching a crew set up for a television show is possibly the dullest thing imaginable. In fact, I don't think it's even imaginable. I have a pretty darn good imagination, and I am confident I can't imagine something that dull. After ten minutes of absolute nothingness—just a lot of unloading of equipment and screwing poles together—we decided to take a silent-TV break. We watched an episode of *Full House* with the closed-captioning on. Twenty-eight minutes later—and the crew still wasn't completely set up.

"TV is boring," I said.

"Hey! Don't make fun of Michelle and D.J. and Joey, and I won't make fun of your Crime Channel addiction," Lily said. Lily proudly claims to have watched *Full House* reruns every week since she was four years old and often talks about the Danny Tanner family as if they were her next-door neighbors.

"I meant that making a TV show is boring," I explained.

"The only thing possibly more boring is watching people make a TV show."

"Let me know when the good stuff starts," Lily said, not taking her eyes off the TV screen as another episode of *Full House* started. I sighed and went back to scoping things out through my camera lens. I moved the lens down the dock until I settled on the golden, shiny head of Monica Heathcliff, the star of *Dockside Blues*, who was in a heated argument with another woman. Both women stood with their hands on their hips, occasionally pointing a hand at the other woman.

I gently eased the window open a crack in the hope of hearing what they were talking about.

"You need to keep your hands out of my business," Monica said.

"It's all over now. They're dead," the other woman said, her voice loud and shrill.

"They're all dead, and there's nothing you can do to bring them back, Celeste."

CHAPTER 12

"CELESTE?" LILY ROLLED off the bed with a thud and crawled to our lookout spot.

Unfortunately, her thudding upstairs disturbed Mango from his peaceful slumber downstairs.

Mango's barking was interrupted by Marcus Dartmouth shouting, "Cut! Cut! Who let a dog stay here during filming? Joshua? Where's Celeste? Wasn't she responsible for clearing everyone out?"

"Oops," Lily said. "I didn't know they were filming yet. Wasn't Monica just yelling at Celeste?"

I sighed. A big, heavy sigh, as if to say, *You have so much to learn.* Then I said, "It appears that 'Celeste' is also the name of a character who was just doing a scene with Monica Heathcliff. A scene that you interrupted."

"Double oops. I thought there was something dead in the water again," Lily replied, and I sighed again dramatically. Clearly Lily needed to watch different television shows to keep up with the real-life show going on below.

"Okay, boy, let's go face the music," I said to Mango. He

wagged his tail, excited to go outside.

"I'm sorry, Mr. Dartmouth, sir," I said as I opened the front door to our cottage. Eight adults were looking directly at me, and not one of them looked happy.

"Marcus! I am exhausted, and I have no patience for continually having to redo scenes out here." Monica Heathcliff looked positively furious. "We need to wrap this up and get out of this waterlogged world and get back to L.A. I insist that you take care of things."

Marcus rolled his eyes and started barking orders for the crew as he walked away.

"Don't you walk away from me," Monica shouted at him. "Come here! Now!"

Hearing those three words, Mango's ears perked up, and he lunged toward Monica.

"Mango! No!" I cried. But it was too late. The dog bounded toward Monica. He's sweet and smart, but he must have honed in on her last few words, thinking she was urgently commanding him to "come here, now."

I charged after him, and Monica threw her hands in the air and started to back away as Mango neared, then jumped up on her.

"Mango! Down! Off! Off!" I couldn't remember if I was supposed to say "down" to get off or "off" to get off. I grabbed him by his collar, but he got up on his hind legs again as if he were dancing with the actress. I had never seen Mango jump up on anyone like that—her hand movements must have been giving him some sort of "up" signal.

Monica continued to stagger backward away from him, and I grabbed for his collar again, shouting, "Down, Mango, down!"

And down he went—pushing the actress who, according to Lily, *People* magazine had recently named one of the Ten Hot New Stars to Watch, with him—and into the water. Unfortunately, my fingers had finally managed to hook his collar, so I went in, too.

"Aaaaarrrgh! Help! Get me out of here! There were dead things in here yesterday!" Monica flailed her arms around, splashing water frantically.

"Here, Miss Heathcliff," I said, treading water. "Take my arm." I bent my arm and held it out so she could steady herself. "Just take a couple strokes down here. There's a ladder." She came along with me, sputtering and spitting and crying all at the same time. Black globs of mascara ran down her cheeks. I guided her to the ladder and then backed up so she could get out first. She was practically hyperventilating she was crying so hard now. "Don't look at me! Don't anyone look at me! That awful dog! He attacked me for no reason!"

"Sorry," I squeaked. "I think he thought you were calling him."

As she climbed up the ladder, Monica bent her arm so that her elbow and forearm covered the top of her face. The TV people stood around gawking at her. Only

Lily ventured forward, helping her up the ladder. Once Monica was all the way up on the dock, she took her arms and covered her chest. Celeste—the *real* Celeste—draped a huge blanket over Monica Heathcliff's shoulders. Two other women guided her off the dock and to one of the trailers out on the street.

Everything was eerily silent. I sensed that the entire cast and crew of *Dockside Blues* were holding their breath.

Marcus Dartmouth's laughter cut through the air like a gas-powered leaf blower roaring into action. "That was priceless! Did you get all of that, Roxy?"

A woman peeked out from behind the camera. "Oh yeah. I got it, all right."

"I couldn't have scripted this better myself. Celeste! I mean the *real* Celeste, the P.A. Celeste! Where are you?" Marcus demanded.

Celeste stepped forward, looking as if she was going to barf.

"Celeste, I want you to find out who owns this dog and get permission for him to join the cast of *Dockside Blues*. You! Up on the dock!"he said, motioning toward me.

Being up on the dock getting chewed out by a TV director was the absolute last place I wanted to be.

Until I turned around and saw the fish. The dead fish.

And then the water was the absolute last place I wanted to be.

"Mango! Let's go, boy!" I said.

CHAPTER 13

"Ick! Ick, ick, ick!" I took six freestyle strokes to the ladder, keeping my head above water. I pulled myself up a couple of rungs, panting heavily. "Come on, Mango! Lily, help me get Mango out of the water! We need to get him out of the water!" I was panicking. If something killed fish, who knows what it could do to Mango. Or to me. Alice had been so adamant that we wash the dog if he got lake water on him. Why hadn't she just told me what was wrong with the water?

My heart seemed to lurch at the same time my brain was whizzing at full speed. Maybe Alice hadn't told us anything specific because she was the one who was doing something weird to the water. No time to think about that. Mango and I had to get clean.

One of the guys who'd unloaded the equipment earlier bent over and effortlessly hauled Mango up on the dock. "Back away!" I commanded. "He's about to shake." Amazingly, people did what I said. Everyone took a couple steps back, as if Mango was some kind of weapon that was going to explode. Mango started to do his predictable wet-dog shake to start getting the water off him.

"There's something wrong with the water here. I just saw dead fish. And Monica saw dead fish yesterday," I explained. Mango sat down and looked at me with his head cocked. "It's okay, boy. We'll get you a bath." I don't know if it was my imagination, but he didn't look too excited about the bath idea.

"Well, I don't see any dead fish," Marcus proclaimed, having glanced over the side of the dock into the water.

"Well, I did!" I said, trying to imitate his tone, with the emphasis on "I," because *I* am just as important as he is.

"You might think you saw dead fish, but it was probably just some plant floating by," Marcus said.

"Monica saw dead fish, too," Lily said, handing a beach towel to me and wrapping a second towel around Mango.

"Monica Heathcliff is an actress. An actress must act. That's what she was doing yesterday—acting," he said.

No one seemed to challenge him on that one. No one was agreeing either.

"I know what I saw," I said, looking directly at Marcus. "There were dead fish in the water, and earlier I saw your parents—"

"Aunt Alice," Marcus said as he quickly turned away from me. "How delightful of you to stop by." He said "aunt" like "aaaaahnt," instead of like "ant." It sounded phony. Then again, this is a guy who calls his mom "mum."

"I live here, Marcus. Or did you forget? I seem to be kicked out of my home while you work on this project of yours." Alice Campbell turned from Marcus and looked directly at me. "Hannah, you need to get into a shower right away. Wash yourself first, and then you girls need to get Mango in the bathtub and give him a thorough shower, too. Here, I brought some special soap for you to use on him."

"Aunt Alice, we're in the middle of something here. I'm sure the girl's and the dog's baths can wait," Marcus said.

"And *I'm* sure they can't wait," Alice said. "You should know that as well as I do." They stared at each other.

I looked from Marcus to Alice. Neither one said anything. Neither one flinched. I was certain that Alice believed something was in the water that wasn't supposed to be there. Something that could kill fish.

And now I had a feeling that Marcus knew, too. I had a feeling Marcus knew exactly what was going on.

"Hannah, I encourage you to get cleaned up," Alice urged me. "I can help you, if you'd like."

"No!" The thought of someone helping me get clean caused instant and thorough mortification. "I mean, no, thank you."

She smiled kindly. "I meant I could help you with Mango. But I know you're an experienced dog washer. Just make sure you rinse him thoroughly. Try to rinse him twice as long as you think is necessary. And be sure to get his belly, his face, and his ears. Inside his ears as well."

Thirty minutes later and Lily was as wet as I was. Washing a dog Mango's size is no easy matter, especially when the usually obedient dog was getting a little testy, seeing as how we were washing him even more thoroughly this time. Alice had me a little alarmed about what chemicals might be in the water at Portage Bay. And let's not forget that I'd actually seen dead fish. Touched dead fish.

Okay, okay. A couple of dead fish in a lake that's sixty miles in diameter may not seem like a big deal. Granted, they weren't even big fish. Just little two-inch fish. I have no idea what kind of fish they were. When I was soaping up in the shower I mulled over whether I should try to scoop up a dead fish and have it analyzed. I nixed that idea when I couldn't think what to do with a dead fish. Look up "fish analysis" in the yellow pages? Google "What killed this fish?"

"We don't even know if there are chemicals in the water," Lily said, moving a blow dryer around Mango. He may not have liked the bath portion of his treatment, but he was pretty happy about the blow dryer. Or maybe he just liked having two girls spend so much time combing and cooing and cuddling him.

"Something's in the water. You saw it, too. The stuff that Marcus's parents put in this morning looked like laundry detergent," I said.

"Maybe it was Tide or Cheer or something," Lily said. "Wouldn't that just clean the water? Tidy it up? Cheer the fish?"

"Oh, come on! Where were you in fourth grade? People can't put detergents and chemicals in the water. It kills things. Maybe even kills fish. Remember when we had to write about that guy in north Seattle who cleaned his driveway with that solvent? The chemicals from his cleaner ran down his driveway, down the hill, and into Lake Washington. He got a huge fine for polluting the water."

"Yeah, I remember," Lily grudgingly agreed.

"And remember when we were in third grade and our field trip to Hood Canal had to be canceled?"

"That was a bummer."

"It was a bigger bummer for the fish that lived there. It was hypoxia, when there isn't much oxygen in the water and it makes these dead zones where deep-water fish can't survive," I said, impressed with my ability to recall the word "hypoxia." Apparently I'd suitably impressed Lily, too.

"I can't believe you remember that. All I remember is that we went to the Children's Museum for about the sixtieth time instead of getting to go to the beach," Lily said.

"Did you hear something?" I asked. Lily turned off the hair dryer. An impatient knocking came at the door.

"Who's there?" I called. It seems kind of stupid to call out like that. It doesn't really protect you from danger. If an ax murderer is on the other side, he isn't exactly going to say, "It's an ax murderer."

"Marcus Dartmouth, director, *Dockside Blues*."

Interesting.

I assumed I'd have my mother's permission to open the door for Alice's nephew, who just happened to be a television producer and director. I opened the door but didn't invite him in. Mom would have my hide if I invited someone into the house when she wasn't there, even if it was a Hollywood director.

"We're going ahead with the shot of you and that dog in the water. I need your parent or legal guardian's permission for you to be on *Dockside Blues*," he said.

Wait a second. Who did this guy think he was, assuming I'd want to be in a primetime television show?

Wait just another second. Who did I think I was, waiting even a second to reply? Oops. Wait again. Lily was the actress. She was the one who wanted a role on this show. How could I be on *Dockside Blues* without my best friend?

"We'll need your friend as well, since she's in the shot where Monica gets out of the water," Marcus said.

Whew, I thought to myself. "Her name is Lily Shannon and my name is Hannah West, and we'll have to talk with our parents to see if we can get their permission. We'll get back to you."

I closed the door.

Lily and I did a silent happy dance, jumping up and down, and mouthing, *We're going to be on TV! We're going to be on TV!*

Mango was not so silent.

CHAPTER 14

IF I THOUGHT watching a TV show being shot was a big snore, I had no idea that having a teensy tiny part on a cable TV series could possibly be so dull either. Here's my advice to actors and actresses everywhere: Bring something to read on the set. Two minutes of glory in front of the camera means eight hours of agony, just sitting around waiting for something to happen.

The worst part was that because my big entrance was done soaking wet, I had to stay soaking wet. I refused to get in the lake water again, so they kept hosing me off. Chet, a guy on the crew, rigged the hose up through a houseboat's outdoor utility sink so at least the water was lukewarm. Still, I was sick of being wet.

Lily and I had called our parents the second we got the big TV news. All responsible adults had agreed that we could participate, and they'd talked to Celeste, the P.A., to verify that they'd sign all the necessary paperwork at the end of the day when they came to Portage Bay.

Lily's dad, Dan, returned from his hundred-mile bike

ride and started to fill out her permission forms.

"I really should have Lily's agent look this over first," he said, handing a stack of papers over to Celeste. Lily and I both groaned at Dan's lame attempt to be funny.

We were each getting a hundred dollars a day. Sounds pretty good, until we found out that tomorrow was going to be our last day. Oh well. That's still two hundred dollars of easy money. That is, if you think it's easy to sit around and be bored and then be wet. Mango was getting the same fee. I volunteered to accept his payment, since I think of myself as his professional handler as well as his walker and his poop picker-upper. But Mom had Celeste take down all of Jake's information for payment.

"You're going to get some mighty nice raw bones there, boy," I said to Mango, giving him a belly rub.

Evenings on the houseboat were wonderful. Everything smelled fresh and clean. It was quiet, especially compared to the way it was during the day with a TV crew on this dock. And with a dog barking. And with an actress screaming.

I looked over the edge of the dock into the water. It didn't *look* dirty or contaminated. It didn't *smell* toxic.

"Let's take out the double kayak," Mom said. She was home after a long shift at Wired Café. She'd taken Mango out for a short jog and was now showered and changed into shorts and a T-shirt.

"I don't know if we should be in the water," I said.

Mom has always said that a big imagination was one of the best things you could have. Would I sound crazy if I told her that I kept seeing people dressed in black scurrying around with buckets and bottles? I don't know if I'd believe myself if I heard that one. But she's my mom, so she kind of has to put up with me. I decided to tell her everything I'd seen in the past few days.

"I'm not sure what Alice has to do with any of this, but remember how we saw her at the island nation of Tui Tui with those glass jars?"I asked.

Mom nodded.

"Well I've seen her a few more times. At first I thought she was putting something into the water, but now I think she's getting samples."

"What do you think she does with those samples?" Mom asked.

"I don't know. But I'm thinking we should get some samples of our own," I said.

"And what do you plan to do with those water samples? Test them in our basement science laboratory?" Mom asked. Geesh. She sounded like an echo of Lily, making fun of me.

"Look over there," I said, pointing across the bay toward the University of Washington. "I bet there's some research lab there that would help us. All we'd need to do is collect the samples."

"Okay. But now you've got me freaked out about what

might be in the water. I hope Alice was overreacting. We should be okay in a kayak. But just in case, let's be extra careful when we gather the water samples," Mom said. She grabbed some Nalgene water bottles from REI and tossed them into a backpack. She tossed in some bagels, grapes, cheese, and bottled water as well. "We might as well have a picnic while we're out there," she said. "We can hose off the kayak as soon as we get back. Just in case."

Just in case there really was something deadly in the water? I was counting on Mom to be calm and rational. She was supposed to balance out my overactive imagination. Suddenly the idea of a picnic on a potential cesspool of water didn't sound too appetizing.

I tossed my essential supplies into a backpack, too. Camera, film, Sharpie, paper, pencil. Everything an amateur sleuth/photographer needs.

This time I let Mom paddle shotgun. In other words, she got the front seat. She pulls harder than I do, anyway, so it's easier to let her be in the lead and do the steering. Otherwise she's a total backseat paddler, telling me to stroke more on the starboard or port side, which doesn't really help get us anywhere any faster because I have to stop and think: starboard means right, port means left. Being in the rear seat makes it easier for me to slack off and take photos, too.

As we reached the middle of the lake and stopped paddling, Mom said, "Now there's a yacht." We were resting and letting the wake in the water bob us along. It felt like a mini-roller-coaster ride every time a big motorboat went by. I followed her gaze right to the *Clean Sweep*. "It's going pretty fast through here, don't you think?"

"Mom, look at the name on that boat," I said. She squinted and took her sunglasses off, but I could tell she couldn't see it clearly. I handed her my camera with the zoom lens. "Oh, my. Is that Marcus's parents' boat? The one you were telling me about?"

"Yep. But remember, it's a *yacht*, not a boat."

"Look, they're slowing down. They must have realized they were speeding." Mom handed the camera back to me. I focused on Timothy, who was wearing his captain's hat. Stella was dropping an anchor. They were close to their yacht club, yet they'd put an anchor down instead of taking their boat into the moorage. I was about to put the camera down when I saw Timothy carry a big white bucket to the side where Stella was. She began scooping something out of the bucket and putting it in the water. I snapped a bunch of pictures, even though I had no idea what I was photographing.

Timothy brought up the anchor, and Stella started the motor. The *Clean Sweep* puttered into the covered docks at the Emerald City Yacht Club.

"Can you keep your eye on the exact spot where they just were?" I asked Mom.

"Got it," she said. "Let's go."

We paddled to the area where the *Clean Sweep* had just been.

"Okay, hand me one of the bottles and I'll get a sample," Mom said.

"Hand you a bottle? What do you mean? You packed the backpack. You have the bottles."

"I saw you bring a backpack," Mom said.

"Right. I brought *my* backpack. You had the other one."

We were silent for a couple of moments. "So, I guess that means that neither one of us has the jars to get a sample. I guess there's only one thing to do." I took out my water bottle.

"Hannah! Don't empty your water right here. If there's anything to be found in a water sample, you might interfere with it," Mom said.

"I wasn't going to," I said. And then I chugged an entire bottle of water.

It was kind of tricky to get a water sample without touching the lake water. In fact, I did get my fingers a little wet.

"Just don't rub your eyes or touch your face," Mom said. That, of course, made my eyes itch like crazy and I had a terrible urge to rub my eyes and my nose and every other inch of my face. "Let's get home as fast as possible."

As soon as we got home, I sat in bed with Mango and the laptop. I went to the Department of Fisheries Web site at the University of Washington and started reading about what different researchers were working on. I had no idea that studying fish could be so incredibly complicated. "Hmmm . . . she sounds promising," I told Mango. Alpha B. Cowlitz got my attention first because of her name, but her university Web site said she was particularly interested in urban waterways and taking action to preserve healthy water quality. Best yet, she had a link from her Web site to a personal Web site that talked about how she loved to kayak and row. In fact, she rowed crew with a recreational team from the university boathouse, conveniently located just across the bay from our dock.

Isn't e-mail great? I get kind of sick of hearing adults complain about how much e-mail they get and how much time it takes. Me? I love it. Especially when I can make myself "look" older through an e-mail message. It gives me extra confidence that I wouldn't have on the phone. No one can tell that I'm just a seventh grader. The trick, you see, is to restrain yourself from trying to sound too much like an adult, which can end up sounding stuffy if you're not careful. Anything too formal or distinguished can be a dead giveaway that you're up to something. Simple and straightforward is what I find works best when you want answers from an adult:

Dear Ms. Cowlitz,

I'm a resident on Portage Bay in Lake Washington near your university. I see that you're interested in urban water issues and I'm wondering if I could enlist your help. I would like to have our water tested. Just a simple test so I won't worry about my puppy, Mango, going for an occasional swim.

Perhaps this will tie in with your own research in some way.

Thank you.

Sincerely,
Hannah J. West

You might notice that I slipped Mango into my query as well. People are suckers for dogs, especially puppies, and I'm sure Mango's youthful personality makes him appear puppylike. I included his name for extra authenticity.

I was Googling "Monica Heathcliff" and "Marcus Dartmouth, director" when my Mac Mail dinged, letting me know I had a new message.

From: Alpha B. Cowlitz

Dear Ms. West,

I'm particularly interested in local urban water quality. I'll be in the lab each day this week from 9 a.m. to 5 p.m. You can call or e-mail me there, or stop by.

She left her lab address and a link to a university map that showed the lab's location on the campus. I whipped out my bus schedules for the number 25 and number 66. Bummer! I'd completely forgotten that I had a television shoot the next day. Oh, it's so hard being a TV star. I had an eight o'clock "call" in the morning. Saving Portage Bay would just have to be put on hold while I pursued my selfish dreams of stardom.

Mango did his tap-dancing routine that meant he had to go relieve himself one last time before turning in for the night.

"Mom, I'm going to the sidewalk to let Mango pee," I called up to the sleeping loft.

"Take a flashlight and come right back," she said.

I'm not easily spooked, but the stillness of the air at night and the lapping sound of the water was kind of creepy. I walked quickly to the little patch of grass that Mango liked to use as his personal bathroom. Luckily, he only peed, and I didn't have to pick anything up. We headed back out the dock when I saw a lantern bobbing out on the water. I could just barely see the outline of a woman in a kayak. I tried to relax my eyes, just like we talk about in art and photography so that I could take in everything a bit easier. See things I hadn't seen before. Well, I saw something I hadn't seen before all right. Alice Campbell was out on the water in a kayak. I could tell from her movements that she was scooping water into bottles and then stowing them in her kayak. I dashed inside and grabbed the camera.

When I came out, I looked through the camera lens and realized it wasn't Alice after all. It was Estie. Out alone in the dark on the water. I took a photograph.

Oops.

Unfortunately, the flash went off. The bright light on a dark night startled me. But not as much as it startled Estie. She screamed as she fell into the water.

I wanted to run back inside and turn off all the lights and pretend that it wasn't me. But what if she was as big of a spaz as Monica Heathcliff in the water?

"Are you okay?" I called out over the water. My voice sounded high and screechy as it interrupted the night.

"I'll be fine," Estie said. She wasn't actually that far out, I realized. It had seemed farther when I'd first spotted her.

"Who's in the water? Does someone need help?" Alice came out of her cottage wearing a fluffy white bathrobe and flip-flops. She looked out at the water. "Oh, dear. Is that you, Estie? Bring the boat back in and come to my house. You can have a nice warm shower, and I'll make you a cup of tea."

Alice turned to me. "Estie asked to borrow my kayak for a little moonlight paddle. I should have asked more about her skills," she said with a slight chuckle.

"I think something startled her out there," I said. Yeah, and that "something" was me and my stupid camera flash.

"I'm sure everything is fine. Good night, Hannah," Alice said. I gratefully went inside, happy that Mango and I were both dry for a change.

But even with Alice's reassurances, I couldn't help but wonder what Estie had really been doing out kayaking in the dark.

CHAPTER 15

MONDAY MORNING I was up early, had the dog walked, my Cap'n Crunch eaten, and my reading material ready when I went to my high-powered television job.

I looked out the window and saw Lily walking out onto the dock. I grabbed my camera off the table—just in case I had a chance to take some pictures of the actors—and headed out the door. "Whew! What a long commute," I announced as I walked out of our houseboat and onto the set.

"Funny," Lily said. "Do I look okay? Do you know what we're going to do today?"

I held up a book called *Lulu Dark Can See Through Walls* in response. I had a feeling I knew exactly what I was going to be doing today: sitting around and reading. And, might I add, making one hundred dollars for my efforts.

"Girls, I'm glad you're here and ready to go," Celeste said. She checked something off a list on her clipboard. "We're going to have to shoot around Monica's scenes today."

"Why?" I asked. I had to keep myself from asking if she

was afraid of the fish-killing toxic water.

"She had to fly back to L.A. Unexpectedly," Celeste said.

"A hair emergency?" I asked. Lily kicked me. "Ow!"

"We have someone to stand in for Monica, and we should be okay as long as we don't get too close," Celeste said.

"Wow. Monica has a double. Who is it?" Lily asked.

"I'd be the last to know. Remember, I'm just the lowly production assistant," Celeste said.

"Tsk, tsk. Don't talk that way." Marcus Dartmouth came up behind Celeste, who immediately turned beet-colored from head to neck. "The P.A. is the most essential person on the crew. Not counting the actors. Or the director. Or the producers, makeup people, writers, continuity director, grips, and camera crew." If he intended a compliment, he certainly failed, as he'd named just about everybody he could possibly name, except for the lunch crew. "Oh, and the caterers. Food people are definitely way up there." Marcus turned around and barked orders to the people setting up the scene.

"And here's our stand-in," he announced proudly. A woman who looked remarkably similar to Monica Heathcliff smiled at everyone. There was something really eerie about her. She could pass as Monica II. Yet something was a little off, most notably the obvious wig of stiff blond hair she was wearing. Her smile went to half-mast.

Bingo!

"Could I take a quick picture?" I asked the new actress. I used my supersweet voice and I was trying to look wide-eyed and easily impressed. Lily looked at me, puzzled. Monica II nodded and the full smile returned to her face. I snapped a photo of Estie Bartlett dressed as Monica Heathcliff.

"Pay attention!" Lily elbowed me back to *Dockside Blues*.

"Your jobs are to act natural," Marcus instructed us. "Act like you live here."

I do live here, I wanted to say.

"We're taking establishing shots first. We'll set the scene with Seattle, some shots from the water, and then some shots of you doing teenage-type things," he continued.

Teenage-type things? Cool! He thought we were teenagers. I was interested to see how they'd stage "teenage-type things."

"Here, start tossing this Frisbee back and forth," Marcus instructed us.

No problem. Both Lily and I are ultimate Frisbee players, so a little dock tossing was supereasy for us. That is, it was supereasy if we were actually paying attention. But it gets a little dull to have people telling you when to smile and how to toss and which way to look and all that. So much for acting naturally. When Marcus instructed me to throw the Frisbee in a totally lame arm movement, I followed his orders and the disc went right over Lily's head and into the water.

"Mango! No!" I said. It was a halfhearted attempt to get him to stop, because truly, I was hoping the dog would do the dogly thing and chew up the Frisbee. A few gnashes with his teeth and the Frisbee wouldn't be worthy of *Dockside Blues*.

"Wait! Mango, no!" This time I really meant no. Because for Mango to get the Frisbee, he'd have to get in the water. Into the icky, scary, possibly contaminated water.

Splash! I had to admit he looked gorgeous going in.

"Brilliant! Simply brilliant! We have yet another shot with the dog in the water. I love it. So authentic," Marcus was going on and on.

"Mr. Dartmouth, I hope you have enough now, because we need to get Mango washed off after being in the lake water," I said, using my superpolite voice.

"Good, good. Yes, get him cleaned up and dried off and we'll shoot it all over again. I want to re-create that last scene down to the smallest detail, but we'll need to start with a dry dog."

Was he serious?

"Actually, I need to get Mango clean and keep him clean," I said.

"You can clean him up, but as I outlined to you earlier, we'll need to go through the sequence of him in the water again," Marcus said.

Here's what I wanted to say next: With all due respect, sir, we cannot let this dog submerge in the lake water again because of unknown contaminants—quite possibly caused by your mother and stepfather—currently in the water. Then I'd take Mango and march confidently toward the end of the dock where I'd go into our gorgeous houseboat and slam the door.

Here's what I said: "Um, I'd better talk with his owner before Mango goes swimming in this water anymore. It might not be good for him."

You can see my dilemma. Okay, two dilemmas. The first is that I'm a total wimp when it comes to direct confrontation. The second is that I'm a total wimp, and I didn't want to get between Mr. Hollywood Hotshot and his Potential Polluter Parents. The only thing I had the guts to stand up for was Mango.

"Fine, fine. I think we have enough. Celeste, take care of these girls. Everyone else, let's break for lunch."

Estie looked completely disappointed that half a day of shooting was over, and she hadn't been in one single scene.

"Come on, Mango," I said to the sopping wet dog. "I think you know the drill." He followed me into the houseboat and into his now familiar bath ritual.

After lunch, Lily, Mango, and I headed up to the bus stop. The Metro bus pulled up right on schedule. I scanned my pass and deposited $1.25 for Mango. "Does your dog need a transfer?" the driver asked, with a smile.

"Sure, thanks."

Lily put her money in. "Her friend needs a transfer, too, please," she said. "It's not fair," she said as she sat down beside me. "Dogs get all the attention."

We got off in the middle of the University of Washington by the Husky Union Building. I waited with Lily until the number 67 came by to take her home. She had to babysit her little brother for the rest of the afternoon. She's not as experienced at riding buses as I am, and I felt kind of protective of her. I wanted to make sure she got on the right one.

As her bus drove away, I pulled out the map I'd printed from the university Web site and headed south through campus to the research building. I started to lead Mango up the steps, and then I spotted the NO DOGS ALLOWED sign hanging on the door. I pulled out my cell phone and called the number Alpha had given me.

"Hello, this is Hannah West. I contacted you about the water in Portage Bay," I said.

"Yes, of course. I'm anxious to meet you," Alpha replied.

"I'm actually right outside of your building, but I have my dog with me. Should I wait for you out here?"

"Wait there and I'll come get you. If you're with me, it won't be any problem to have a dog inside."

A few seconds later a thin woman with long black hair in a ponytail came out. She looked at us and kept looking. She looked again. Mango was, after all, the only dog around.

"Excuse me, are you Hannah?" she asked.

"Yes, I am." I tried to look older than seventh grade. Who was I trying to impress? This woman was wearing a Hello Kitty T-shirt.

"Sorry, I thought you'd be older," she said.

"I thought you would be, too," I countered.

"I'm old enough," she said a little defensively. "I'm twenty-five."

"This is Mango," I said, hoping to get on her good side with my cute dog. "He's the reason I'm worried about the water quality in the lake."

She looked at us again and then sighed and said, "Come inside and we can talk." Mango and I followed her into the brick research building, down a flight of stairs, and through a long hallway painted a garish blend of green and yellow. "I share an office with another graduate student, but he's not here right now." She moved a stack of papers off of a wood chair and gestured for me to sit down.

"I brought a water sample I took yesterday," I said. I took my Talking Rain bottle out of my messenger bag and set it down. I'd used a Sharpie to write the time and date on the bottle. I pulled out a map of Portage Bay and handed it to her, too. "I marked the spot where I got the water. Or at least the general area."

"Why did you choose this particular spot to take a water sample? Is this where your dog likes to swim? It seems pretty far from shore."

"Um, actually, this isn't where he swims. My mom and I were kayaking last night when we got this sample," I started to explain.

"Why this spot?"

"Well, we saw a suspicious-looking boat in the area, and we wanted to see what they were up to. I thought maybe they were dumping something in the water," I said.

"Or they could be, like you, trying to get water samples to study." Why was this woman challenging me on this? Maybe Alpha B. Cowlitz was not the kind of researcher who wanted to help a kid. Maybe her interest in healthy urban waterways was tied to wealthy urban donors. Maybe she'd thought I was an adult with lots of money, based on where I said I lived. I had only one more trick up my sleeve. Honesty.

"Listen, my mom and I are house-sitting on a houseboat on Portage Bay. I've seen some weird things that make me wonder about the water, including some little dead fish right off our dock. I looked through newspaper archives and couldn't find any stories about anything being dumped in the water. There haven't been any warnings not to swim. But there's definitely something strange going on."

Alpha seemed to relax and get more interested in my problem. Maybe she could see that I was serious.

"Hannah, you said you live on a houseboat. Can you give me an exact address?"

I gave it to her, and after she wrote it down she went to

a tall metal file cabinet and pulled out a file.

"Have you talked to any of your neighbors about this?" she asked.

"No. Not yet."

"Hannah, I won't be able to test your water sample," she said.

Drat! I thought I had her. But she kept talking.

"I'll have to get my own water samples and do it systematically and scientifically. Not that you did anything wrong. You did a great job with the general location and the date and time. But I'll need more specific information."

"Does this mean you'll help me?" I asked.

"I will. This ties directly into my own research project."

"Do you think that yachts might be involved in polluting the water?" I asked.

"I can't tell yet. I can tell you that it's not just a case of gasoline-powered engines and their exhaust causing the trouble. I do have a hunch that power boats are involved, however," she said.

Boats involved, but not because of their engines? I wished she would tell me more, but she insisted she needed to do some tests first.

"And before we take this any further, there's someone else I think you should talk to," Alpha said.

"Who?"

"Alice Campbell."

CHAPTER 16

MANGO AND I got back to the dock while the crew was still filming. I plopped down on the sidewalk by the mailboxes and tried to figure out what to do.

"Aren't they done yet?" Alice asked as she wandered back toward the dock. Just the person I wanted to see. Especially since Alpha had just mentioned her.

"Nope. They're still here," I said, stating the obvious.

"Well, I was planning on going home, but luckily I'm dressed for my daily walk," Alice said, gesturing at her black tracksuit. Mango barked when he heard the word "walk."

"That's right, I love to walk, don't I?" Alice said, obviously enjoying egging Mango on. "I walk four miles every day." He barked each time she said "walk." Alice laughed each time he barked. "I think Mango would like to accompany me," she said. "Would you like to join us?"

Of course I wanted to go on a walk with her. This was the perfect chance to ask her what she'd been up to. I was going to be smooth, though, and follow her lead about the right time to start asking questions. I'd warm her up. Get her talking about other things. I'd let her set the pace.

Alice also set the pace for walking. And what a pace. Yowza. You can never tell how hilly a place is until you're on your feet or pedaling a bike. We had maybe two blocks of flat streets, and then we went up a supersteep hill that had ridges in the sidewalk to keep people from toppling over when they came down. Alice walked fast—and I do mean fast. It was hot, and I was hot. "Do you always walk this fast? For the whole four miles?" I asked.

"We'll only go a couple miles this afternoon," she said. "But to answer your question, I like to walk fast. I ran until I was fifty-three. Arthritis in my knee slowed me down to a walk."

"I wouldn't call this slow," I said, huffing as we entered a dense, shady forest. "Wow. Where are we? Is this some kind of park?"

"Not just any park. This is a historical section of Seattle," Alice began. "Imagine this at the turn of the century. Make that the turn of the twentieth century, more than one hundred years ago. Bicycles and horses and buggies were favored forms of transportation then. This park was designed as a bicycle boulevard linking downtown and Capitol Hill to the shores of Lake Washington. At one time these pathways were filled with cyclists on their way to picnics or to work."

I could totally imagine it. Wide paths meandered up

the steep face of Capitol Hill, with lush forest growth on each side of the paths, making it shady and cool. I suppose the trees could even protect bicyclists from the rain. They were that thick.

"I can't imagine riding up this without a twenty-four-speed bike," I said.

"You'd have to stand up on your pedals and work your muscles hard," Alice said. "Of course, there's no shame in getting off a bike and walking it uphill either. But you'd want to stay on your bike for the downhill ride. It must have been exhilarating."

"This is so cool! And it must smell really good, too," I said. Mango was sniffing around like crazy.

"I like to bring people here so that others will realize what a treasure we have in this park. We still have fifty-one acres here."

"Do you think we're in danger of losing it?" I asked, feeling a bit panicky.

"Oh, there's always that chance. This is prime real estate. But it's also an important part of Seattle's history. Part of the city's legacy. Some of our most gorgeous parks, including this one, are thanks to the Olmsted brothers, sons of the man who designed New York's Central Park."

I was quiet for a while, mostly because we were going up such a steep incline.

"Whoa! What's that?" I asked as we approached a tall brick structure. It towered over the trees ahead of us. "I had no idea a place like this existed in Seattle."

"It's now the Seattle Hebrew Academy. It was first built in 1916 as a convent. It was situated here, by Interlaken Park, to be far from the wicked ways of Seattle proper. It's a gorgeous building, isn't it?"

"I wonder if the nuns liked living there," I said.

She stopped walking and looked directly at me.

"I wonder if you're wondering about something else," Alice said.

"Well, actually, I am."

"I told you earlier, if you're wondering about something, all you have to do is ask," she said.

Here goes: "Who are you trying to protect?" I blurted out.

CHAPTER 17

ALICE STARTED WALKING again without answering me. She seemed intent on watching the pathway as we wound our way back down the steep hills of Interlaken Park.

"It's Marcus, isn't it?" I prodded.

Still no answer.

"Marcus's parents are doing something weird to the water. And you're trying to cover for them. You're not just covering for them, though. You want to make sure that Marcus isn't hurt by what they're doing."

"No, that isn't it," Alice said. She sounded much older and more tired than when she was giving me the historic tour of the park.

"So you're not trying to protect him?" We were going downhill, heading back toward Lake Washington and the Portage Bay dock.

"It's complicated, Hannah."

"If something is in the water that can kill fish, we have to stop it, no matter how complicated it is," I said. I couldn't help it when an argumentative tone crept into my voice. But this was big-time stuff.

"I agree with you completely, Hannah. We need to stop whatever is going on," Alice said.

"Then let's stop it!" I said adamantly. "Mom has a friend at KOMO TV. We can call her once we get Alpha's water test results. We can go to the city council and the newspapers."

"You know Alpha?" Alice asked. She'd looked so serious just moments ago, but now she smiled. "My, you do get around, don't you?"

"The thing is, I still don't know what's going into the water or why it's going in," I said.

"There's still a lot I need to sort out,"Alice said. Then she went into silent mode for the rest of our walk back to the dock.

Alpha Cowlitz, the university researcher, was just getting off the bus when Alice and I got back down to Boyer Avenue.

"Alpha!" Alice called. "It's wonderful to see you. Although I can't say I'm surprised. We were just talking about you."

Alice invited Alpha and me into her cottage. She put a bowl of water down for Mango, who lapped it up sloppily and then lay down on the cool kitchen floor.

"Alice, I told Hannah that I need to do systematic testing to get any reliable readings on the water quality here," Alpha began. "But I couldn't resist doing some preliminary tests on the samples you gave me already."

"Before you go any further, I want to give Hannah a bit of background," Alice said. "Residents on this part of Lake Washington, here in Portage Bay, have a long history of fighting for clean water."

Here we go again, I thought. I might as well put all questions on hold until Alice gave me another Seattle history lesson.

"It's almost impossible to believe," Alice continued, "but back in the 1970s the city of Seattle used to actually dump raw sewage into the water here."

"Gross!" I couldn't help interrupting.

"Yes, it's gross. And unconscionable. One would think that we would have learned by now to be careful what we put in the water. Still, there are people living in big houses who use toxic chemicals to clean their driveways and patios, and then hose off the cleaner, and the runoff then gets into our lakes and streams.

"In the early summer I noticed that some of the plant life in the lake seemed to be particularly robust. We had an unusually dry and warm spring, as you might recall. When I was kayaking, I'd often find my paddle hitting a plant or bringing up plant material. Then, about two weeks ago, I realized that I'd had several kayak sessions without encountering any aquatic plants. And of course that ridiculous actress saw those dead fish."

"I'm not surprised that the aquatic plants have receded,"

Alpha said. "I've noticed the same thing when I'm rowing from the Pocock Center at the university. It makes perfect sense with what I found in the water samples."

Alice and I looked at Alpha, waiting for her to continue. "What did you find?" Alice prodded.

"Herbicides."

"Herbicides?" I asked.

Alpha explained that certain types of plants in the lake could actually take root on boats—a fact that didn't go over so well in the yachting community.

It all started to make sense. They weren't trying to kill fish. They were trying to kill plants.

Lily's lame joke from earlier in the week echoed in my head. She'd said: "Maybe it was Tide or Cheer or something. Wouldn't that just clean the water? Tidy it up?" In a twisted way, she was right. Because someone had the extra-twisted idea of dumping herbicides in the water so that those big expensive boats would be cleaner.

Chapter 18

"I GOT THESE developed for you," Mom said, handing me three packages of developed film. "They're on this CD, too."

"You're the best mom ever!" I said, snatching the envelopes from her.

"Does that mean you want to come with me tonight when I go back downtown to review an art opening?" she asked.

"Actually, it doesn't mean that at all. But you're still the best. As long as you let me stay home and go kayaking tonight," I said. "I need to get some more photos to fill in a couple of gaps here." I spread my new black-and-white photos across the kitchen table, organizing them as I went. I had the pictures of Stella and Timothy on the *Clean Sweep*, the shot of Estie night kayaking, and many more. As I looked through them, more and more pieces of the puzzle started to come into focus, so to speak. But there were still a few things I didn't fully understand.

"If we get up early, you and I can kayak tomorrow morning," Mom said. "But you are not allowed to take

Jake's boat out alone. I'm glad he has a double kayak so you won't be tempted," she added. "But even if he had a single, you are not to go out alone. I repeat: You, Hannah West, may not go out on the water alone tonight. Or at any other time. Understood?"

"I understand you perfectly," I said. I stormed off to my temporary bedroom with Mango right at my heels. It's hard to sulk properly with an adorable labradoodle, so I curled up on the bed with the pooch and did some online research about aquatic plants. After Mom left, I got my camera out anyway and headed outside. Through the telephoto lens I saw a woman with long blond hair emptying a garbage pail into the water from a small motorboat.

Click. Refocus. Advance the film. *Click.* This was great stuff! It might not have anything to do with herbicides, but it reminded me of those nuts in the 1970s dumping sewage into the lake. This woman was emptying an entire garbage can! *Click.* There's no way she could have heard me—I was a hundred yards away—but she looked up and directly into the camera. Monica Heathcliff! I could see the headline right above my photo: "Famous Hollywood Actress Litters in Lake—photos by Hannah West." I zoomed in again and caught her mouth in a position that I recognized. It wasn't Monica after all. It was Estie. Just like that, my dreams of selling my photos to *Hollywood Star* evaporated.

I kept snapping anyway.

Splash. I took my eye from the viewfinder and saw

Alice Campbell taking her kayak in the water. The usually graceful Alice wasn't typically a splasher, but she was definitely in a hurry. She stroked strong and deep, making incredible speed for a human-powered boat.

She was heading right for where I'd seen Monica Heathcliff. Or was she heading to the boat nearby? I looked through the camera again.

The *Clean Sweep* was crisply framed in my viewfinder.

I slung the camera strap around my neck and clumsily got Jake's kayak down and into the water. I looked around, hoping one of the other neighbors might be around. I was itching to get on the water, but I'd promised I wouldn't go out alone.

Turns out someone else was itching to get on the water.

Thud. I turned back to the kayak.

"Mango! How did you get in there, boy?"

Sitting in the backseat of Jake Heard's double kayak was his dog. He obviously wanted to go for a ride . . . and that meant I wouldn't be alone. Maybe this was exactly why Jake had a double in the first place.

"Okay, Mango, you're on!" I grabbed a paddle and eased quickly into the front spot of the kayak. My strokes weren't as deep or as quick as Alice's were, but I made amazingly good time out into the water. Monica Heathcliff's boat must have motored off, but Alice was almost out to the *Clean Sweep*. I had a great view, so I pulled to a stop and fiddled with the camera until Alice, Timothy, and Stella were all in view. Stella leaned over the side of the boat, talking earnestly to Alice below. Alice began raising out of the kayak, as if she were going to pull herself onto the yacht. Stella leaned over further and—

"Alice!" I screamed.

But she was already in the water. I'd captured her tumble into the water on film. I thought Stella had pushed her, and I was pretty sure I'd have a photo to prove it. But there was no more time for photos. I started stroking as fast as I could toward the *Clean Sweep*, with Mango announcing our arrival in a series of quick barks.

"Alice!" I called out. She was now up in the boat, and Timothy had draped a blanket around her wet shoulders. Stella was crying. And Alice was crying.

"I'm so sorry," Alice said.

"No, no, I'm so sorry that we suspected you," Stella said. Huh?

CHAPTER 19

FIFTEEN MINUTES LATER, Mango and I were aboard a gigantic yacht pleasure cruising toward the Emerald City Yacht Club. Stella and Timothy had rushed Alice back to her houseboat so she could take a shower. While she got thoroughly clean, Stella had called Maggie on her cell phone to ask if I could accompany Alice as their guests to the yacht club.

I was trying to be patient, but there was still so much to know. Still, this was my first time on a pleasure-cruising yacht, and I was determined to enjoy the ride.

"This is the life, isn't it, boy?" I said. Mango licked my face and then stretched his head over the side of the boat, just like a dog does in a car when the windows are down.

"I didn't completely suspect you, Alice," Stella was saying when I joined everyone inside the yacht. And I do mean "yacht." This thing was like a house with a motor. I wanted to snoop around and see what was downstairs, but the conversation up above was just too good to miss. "It's just that I know you'd do anything to protect Marcus.

You were always so special to him, and I know you adore him, too." Stella and Alice hugged, and Timothy stood by with a big smile on his face.

"If you two aren't dumping herbicides in the water, who is?" I asked.

Timothy's smile instantly disappeared. "Why on earth would you think that Stella and I would put something toxic into the water?" he demanded.

"Um, well," I stammered. "You see, I had this theory going . . ."

"Let's hear this theory," Timothy said.

No way was I going to tell him what I was thinking. But then his smile returned, and it seemed like a genuine, kind smile.

"You won't hurt our feelings, Hannah. I just really want to know."

"Um, you see, I first thought that it was something emitted from the engine or the fuel used in motorboats. But that wasn't it. But I couldn't get the name of your boat out of my head."

"The *Clean Sweep*?" Stella asked.

"Yeah. *Clean Sweep*. I had a feeling you both liked your boat to be superclean. And maybe that's why you named it the *Clean Sweep*," I said.

"I do like a clean ship," Timothy said.

"But that's not the reason for the name," Stella added.

"I was just guessing. Alice said something about how

her paddle kept getting caught in the plants growing in the lake. I thought maybe somehow the plants were interfering with your boat, too. I mean, your yacht."

"That's a pretty good theory," Timothy said.

"But it turns out to be wrong," Stella added.

"I can tell you about the name *Clean Sweep*," Alice said. "I bet Alpha could have guessed it as well. Timothy was a rower in college."

"We made a clean sweep my senior year, taking the national championship from Harvard," Timothy said.

"Did you say something back there about Alpha?" Stella asked. "Such a beautiful but unusual name. Timothy, isn't that the name of the woman we met at Stephen's lab?"

"Who's Stephen?" Alice and I both asked at the same time.

"He's a graduate student over at the university. He developed the herbicide neutralizer we were testing," Timothy said.

"The what?" Alice and I asked in unison again.

"We're trying to counteract the effects of the chemicals that are attacking the aquatic plant life. We were hoping for an easy fix, but we had no idea that the herbicides would be toxic enough to kill fish as well. The problem is a lot bigger than we first thought," Stella said.

"Why didn't you try to find and stop the polluter instead of covering it up?" I asked. But no one said anything. I wondered if they were afraid to answer. Maybe they didn't want to say that Marcus was the one they suspected. I could tell that Alice didn't want to say that Marcus, her own nephew, was the one she suspected (although it had already come out that Alice suspected Marcus's loving parents of helping him with the scheme). None of the adults wanted to say it, so no one said anything for a while.

"I don't think it was Marcus," I said, interrupting the silence. They all looked at me but were still silent. "Really. I don't think he's behind this. Have you ever asked him?"

They shook their heads.

"By this time tomorrow, I think I can prove who was behind it," I said with a bit more confidence than I actually felt. The adults didn't look as if they had much confidence in me either.

"Alice, does the Floating Home Association have meetings?" I asked.

"Yes, of course. We have one the day after tomorrow," she said. "It's at my house."

"Do you think you could have it somewhere else instead?" I asked. "That is, of course, if the yacht club would let us."

CHAPTER 20

IT TURNED OUT that Stella Dartmouth was a vice president of the yacht club, in line to be commodore next year. Scheduling a meeting at the yacht club was no problem when a VP makes the call.

I made sure that Alpha and Stephen, the other researcher, could come to the meeting. Stella invited Marcus. Alice enticed everyone on our dock—plus Lily—to come by offering a free dinner at the yacht club after the meeting. People who had lived near the yacht club for years said they'd never actually been invited inside. Mom called her friend Mary Perez at KOMO TV. If things didn't play out the way I thought they would, Mary could still do a feature story about the Floating Home Association.

"You can add houseboats to the list of stories that people can't resist," Mary said. "Other parts of the country can count only on cute kids and puppies to lure in viewers no matter what. In Seattle, we have kids, puppies, and houseboats."

"Look! It's Monica Heathcliff!" someone said. A woman

with blond hair entered the lobby of the Emerald City Yacht Club, creating quite a stir.

"Can't they tell it isn't Monica?" I asked Lily. "That hair color is so obviously fake."

Lily looked at me in disbelief. "And you thought that the real Monica had natural-looking hair? If we hadn't met Monica, if we'd seen her only on TV and in *People* magazine, I bet we'd think this was the real thing."

"Oh, I think we could see through to Estie Bartlett," I said.

"Doubt it," Lily said in a singsong voice.

"Girls, the meeting is about to begin," Alice said.

"Are you nervous?" I asked.

"Not about the meeting. Not even about the TV camera," Alice said. "But I am a bit nervous about the lines you've given me."

"I bet the magic of being around *Dockside Blues* will make you an Emmy Award-winning actress in your own right," Lily said.

"I hope you're right," Alice said. She went up to the front of the room to begin the meeting.

"Before we go through our business agenda, I'd like to introduce a few special guests and make an exciting announcement," Alice said to the group of about thirty people gathered in a meeting room called the Captain's Room. She introduced Alpha Cowlitz and Stephen Vargas as two "bright young researchers committed to the environment and healthy water." She introduced Stella and Timothy Dartmouth as "our gracious hosts today, who are eager for Emerald City Yacht Club to become more involved in our neighborhood."

"And now I'd like to introduce our special guest, Monica Heathcliff," Alice said. Everyone clapped enthusiastically. Estie was caught off guard at this announcement, but by the time the camera had turned toward her and the applause started, she was tossing her hair and acting as confident as if she really were a Hollywood star.

"Monica is suffering from a bit of voice strain today," Alice looked pointedly at Estie, who obligingly touched her neck as if she might have a sore throat. "She's asked me to go ahead and make her exciting announcement." Alice paused for drama before continuing, "I feel so privileged to tell you that Monica Heathcliff and her sister, Estie Bartlett, have begun a Portage Bay Stewardship program to ensure that we have healthy, clean water for decades to come." There was spontaneous applause. The next moment was a true test of Estie's acting abilities. She looked stunned. Confused. Angry. And then, magically, she smiled radiantly and nodded. Again her fingers went to her neck and her supposed sore throat. "In addition, these two environmentally conscious sisters will be working with the Emerald City Yacht Club and boating groups to spread the word about healthy water and safe boating." Alice continued with a list of all the commitments we'd dreamed up for Estie.

I passed a small notebook with photos to Estie.

"What's this?" she asked out of the side of her mouth.

"It's just a little motivation to help you remember why you are so committed to the cleanup effort here on Portage Bay," I said. Estie grimaced as she turned the pages. "Nice close-up," I added as she got to the photos I'd taken of her pouring something into the water off the dock, pouring something into the water from a kayak. "You can imagine how excited I was to find such a famous actress in the background of some of my shots."

Estie just nodded and continued smiling.

I'd managed to zoom in pretty well on Estie's face in those shots. What I hadn't expected was the bonus of finding her in eight of my other pictures. I'd taken the digital files and enlarged them in Photoshop. That's when I noticed a woman with long blond hair in a boat near the subject of my shots. I considered them extra insurance. Estie might possibly claim that she was just helping investigate water problems by gathering water samples. However, these shots clearly—or at least somewhat clearly—showed her pouring a powdered substance into the water.

Sitting through the business meeting of the Floating Home Association wasn't exactly exciting, but I bet it was even tougher for Estie to sit through it all.

CHAPTER 21

"THIS KIND OF litter patrol totally rocks!" Lily said, moving from side to side so that our double kayak was actually rocking.

"Stop it or I'm going to have to send you to shore patrol," I said. Our job was to paddle around and look for any floating soda cups, beer cans, plastic bags, and other trash that might have landed on the water.

Monica Heathcliff—the real Monica Heathcliff—and her brown-haired sister Estie Bartlett were picking up trash on the shore and surrounding neighborhood. About twenty other people had shown up as part of the Portage Bay Stewardship Cleanup Day.

It turns out I really did have photos of a famous actress littering. I spent more time in Photoshop cleaning up and enlarging and found that there were actually two different women in the backgrounds of some of the photos. Five of the photos had Estie, but three had Monica, who, it turns out, had enlisted Estie's help. In return, Monica promised to help her sister get a role in a television show.

"Why would Monica be interested in polluting water up here?" Marcus had asked me at dinner the night we committed Monica and Estie to being environmental advocates.

"I wasn't sure at first, either," I admitted. "I found a photo of her in *People* with a guy who is supposedly in real estate in Seattle, according to the caption."

"That would be Harrison Donegal," Marcus said. "They're engaged."

"Harrison? Is that the fellow who recently joined the yacht club?" Timothy asked his wife.

"I believe it is," I answered for Stella. "I found out that he owns a thirty-two-foot boat but has just ordered a new sixty-footer that's going to be delivered next month."

"He wanted the plants cut back for his new luxury yacht," Alice said.

"Yep," I said.

Harrison Donegal wasn't on hand to pick up trash. I'd have to find some other way to make sure that he paid for what he did. Alice and her neighbors assured me they could think up some sort of charitable task for him to take on.

"I still don't get why you guys didn't just expose the people who were dumping the herbicides," Lily said.

"Alice tried contacting someone to take action or to charge them with polluting or illegal dumping. Everything is a big mess because there are at least five towns that border the lake plus the Archipelago of Tui Tui, and they're not sure which one of them will press charges. It could take months—or longer—for them to get it all straightened out," I said.

"That's gross. They're getting off way too easy," Lily said.

"The story isn't over. Look, there's Mary!" I waved to Mom's friend the television reporter, who had a camera woman with her today. She was getting some footage to round out her story about illegal dumping. Alpha had already given her preliminary water test results to Mary. I didn't know if my photos would play any role or not, but at least I had them in case anyone decided to charge Estie and Monica with some kind of crime.

"Hey, Hannah," said Polly Summers, Mom's friend who had just paddled up in a kayak with her husband, Tom. As avid kayakers, they were helping to clean up the bay as well. "I just told your mom that I got a lead on someone in Fremont who needs a live-in dogsitter while she goes to Hong Kong for a business trip. You could be living in—"

"The Center of the Universe!" I finished for her. Fremont is this funky, artsy Seattle neighborhood that decided to name itself the Center of the Universe. If I could walk on water living in Portage Bay, who's to say I can't journey to the Center of the Universe?

Q and A

with NANCY PEARL

and LINDA JOHNS

NANCY PEARL: Where did the inspiration for the Hannah West books come from?

LINDA JOHNS: My favorite mysteries are stories set in real places, like *Harriet the Spy*, which takes place in New York City. My favorite city is Seattle, where I've lived most of my life. I wanted to write a mystery story that was set in Seattle, but it didn't all start coming together until I had the character of Hannah West in my head.

I needed a way for Hannah to be in different parts of the city so she could solve mysteries. I knew she also needed some sort of "cover," a way to be out and about observing things. A good detective is always observing. Walking a dog is a great way to explore new neighborhoods, and it seemed natural that Hannah, a dog lover, would have a dogsitting and dog walking business. If Hannah and her mom were also professional house sitters, they'd have a chance to live in fancy places and meet all kinds of interesting people. And all of this gave me the opportunity to spend countless hours walking my dog, Owen, around funky and charming neighborhoods.

NP: Why did you choose to make Hannah Chinese?

LJ: I based the character of Hannah on one of my favorite girls, who happens to have been born in China and adopted by an American family. I hadn't read many books for young readers that represented the people I know and see every day. And I didn't know of any books, at that time, with a main character who was Chinese-born and adopted as a baby and brought to the US.

NP: When you wrote the first book, *Hannah West in the Belltown Towers*, did you think you'd write three more about the same character? Do you ever think about writing more about Hannah and her friend Lily?

LJ: I'm very attached to Hannah as a character and I hoped that I'd be able to write more stories starring Hannah solving mysteries. I wrote and rewrote the first mystery several times, with lots of edits and tweaks in each new version, before I sent it to my agent. I wrote a brief overview about two more potential mysteries. I was thrilled to get to write not just two, but three more. I am sure there are more mysteries that need to be solved in Seattle, and I think Hannah and her best friend Lily are the duo to do it.

NP: When did you know you wanted to be a writer? Did you write stories as a child? If so, do you still have some of them? How do you feel reading them now?

LJ: I was in second grade when I decided I wanted to be a writer. My mom kept the story that set me on this path. It was really sweet of her to keep it, and it was also indicative of how much both my parents supported me as a writer. In fact, every job I took as an adult, my mom would always ask, "Are you sure you'll have enough time to keep writing?" But back to my second grade story: It would have been better with more action. It still delights me to remember how much fun I had writing it.

NP: Do you like to read? What sorts of books? As a child, were you a big reader? How did (or not) your parents encourage you to read? What were some of your favorite books as a kid?

LJ: I love to read! Right now I tend to read mysteries and general fiction. I read books written for children, teens, and adults. I'm from a family of readers, and it was a common occurrence to see my parents and my sister and I all together in the living room, each a world away in a book. We were definitely a family that took "reading together" to heart. My parents encouraged me to read whatever caught my fancy. Sometimes that meant sitting next to a set of encyclopedias and flipping through the pages. The "D" encyclopedia was my favorite because it was the one with several pages on dog breeds and their history.

At my elementary school, once we were in fourth grade, our daily reading time was spent in the library reading whatever we wanted. How great is that? Almost an entire hour each day at school where you could sprawl out on the floor or curl up in a chair and read. I claimed the "H" aisle in the library as my reading spot because that's where Marguerite Henry (she wrote horse books, like *Misty of Chincoteague)* was. I read my way through the library, choosing a book from each section. Whenever we finished a book, we'd sit down with our librarian, Ms. Elrod, and talk to her about what happened in the book and what we liked about it. A lot of who I am now is grounded in those hours in the library and the conversations with Ms. Elrod.

When I was younger, I loved the picture book *Harry the Dirty Dog* by Gene Zion, illustrated by Margaret Bloy Graham. My friend Hannah (who is a librarian) gave me a Harry the Dirty Dog T-shirt for a recent birthday and I am so happy whenever I wear it.

NP: If someone liked your books, what others would you recommend?

LJ: Try the Gilda Joyce mystery series by Jennifer Allison. Gilda is a psychic investigator who often underestimates how her own intelligence is what's actually solving a mystery. She's a resourceful spy and has a flair for disguises when she needs to go undercover. And don't miss *The Wig in the Window* by Kristen Kittscher, starring best friends Sophie Young and Grace Yang as unstoppable young detectives. *The Westing Game* by Ellen Raskin is an older mystery (published in 1978) that I think stands the test of time. It features a young detective piecing together clues to solve a rock-solid mystery. *The Westing Game* is my all-time favorite mystery, and that includes the adult mysteries I've read as well.

NP: I know that you're a librarian—is that a good career choice for someone who likes to read and write stories?

LJ: Being a librarian is a perfect job for someone who loves reading and writing! In addition to getting to be around books and talk about books, a librarian spends a lot of time working directly with people and hearing their stories. A big part of being a writer (or a detective!) is observing people and tracking down information. A librarian gets to do this every day, a hundred times each day.

I had a great professor at the University of Washington who inspired many of my coworkers and I to be librarians. Her name was Nancy Pearl and she taught us that there is a book for every reader. If you can get someone to talk about a book he or she has loved, you can pick up clues to find the right book at the right moment for that reader. Writers, detectives, and librarians—we all use clues, stories, and information to save the day.

ABOUT the AUTHOR

LINDA JOHNS is a writer, reader, and librarian. The order changes depending on the day. She works at the Seattle Public Library's downtown Central Library, a gorgeous eleven-story building with a million books inside. She grew up in Cheney, Washington, and graduated from Washington State University with a degree in journalism. She has a master's degree in library and information science from the University of Washington. Her first job, at age fifteen, involved a lot of stapling. Subsequent jobs (after college) included reporter, editor, and bookseller. Linda lives in Seattle with her husband, son, and a basset hound named Owen Henderson.